Texas
CHRISTMAS BRIDES

Texas CHRISTMAS BRIDES

*Two Delightful Stories
of New-to-Town Women
Who Each Become Targets of
Matchmaking Schemes*

KATHLEEN Y'BARBO & CATHY MARIE HAKE

BARBOUR
PUBLISHING

Published by Barbour Publishing, Inc., P.O. Box 719, Uhrichsville, Ohio 44683, www.barbourbooks.com

Our mission is to publish and distribute inspirational products offering exceptional value and biblical encouragement to the masses.

ecpa Member of the
Evangelical Christian
Publishers Association

Printed in the United States of America.
5 4 3 2 1

Prologue

by Kathleen Y'Barbo

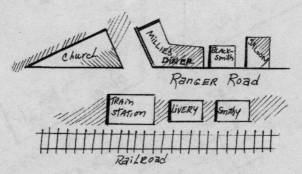

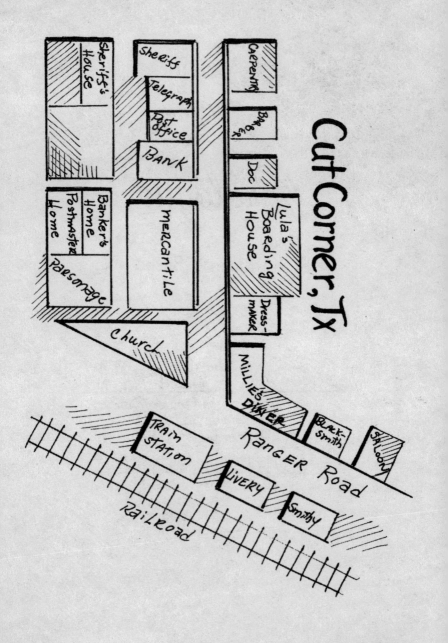

Prologue

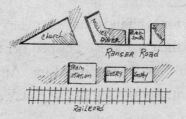

San Antonio, Texas
Christmas Day, 1851

Texas Ranger captain Ebenezer "Eb" Wilson swiped at his eyes with the back of his hand and knelt at Carolina's bedside. On the other side of the closed door, his firstborn, Rafael Ebenezer, wailed in the capable arms of his grandmother. His wife had given him a strong, fine son, a lad with his mama's dark hair and his papa's talent for howling at full volume.

If only he'd been there when. . .

"Eb, promise me. . . ."

Jerking his attention back to the tiny form beneath the

blankets, Eb felt the tears threaten again. His beautiful fiery wife, the delicate counterpoint to his big, clumsy self, lay so still and pale that he barely recognized her. The very life seemed to flow from her as the clock at the bedside ticked.

She reached for his hand, but her fingers fell limp on the quilt just shy of their mark. Eb grasped her tiny hand in his and lifted it to his lips. "Anything, Lina. Anything."

For a moment, fire flashed in Carolina's eyes, a reminder of the saucy senorita he'd met and married in a whirlwind courtship barely one year ago. "Don't let my mama take our Rafael to raise. Get him another mama, someone young and strong who'll love him like me."

"No." The sharpness of his tone startled him, but it seemed to have no effect on Carolina. "I'll never marry again. I–I couldn't."

Her fingers slid from his grasp to wipe a tear off his cheek. "Then I will only pray you will consider it."

"I'll try, but you'll be everywhere I look. How's a man going to find a new wife like that?" His poor attempt at humor fell flat, but Carolina, bless her soul, chuckled anyway.

"Leave San Antonio then," she said softly. "The city is no place to raise a child."

"Maybe I will, Lina," he said, although he had no idea

how he, a ranger captain, would ever settle somewhere and raise a baby. His life and his command were here. So was the extended family that would help him care for his son. People like Lula Chamberlain and Millie, his wife's best friends, would never let him leave.

Right now, however, he would promise her the moon and all the stars in the sky if she asked. Setting up housekeeping somewhere quiet and raising a baby seemed minor in comparison. "It might take me some time," he amended. "A man has to plan these things."

"You and your plans. Do you think I don't hear you and your friends when you speak of the things you will do when you are no longer rangers?" She caught his gaze, and her eyes narrowed. "Find some land. Start a little settlement up north where the weather's cooler. Put down roots someplace nice and safe from the *banditos*. Did you and those three *compadres* of yours not say this?"

"Well now, we might have mentioned it a time or two."

Indeed, he and fellow rangers Stone, Swede, and Chaps had jawed about doing just that for a while now. They even had a name for their little town: Cut Corners, Texas. Of course, that was just fool talk, part jest and part wishful thinking. He hadn't actually thought about the reality of it, and he doubted the other three had either.

"Then make your Cut Corners a reality, *mi amour*. Promise me."

"I promise." He paused to add a dash of reason to the statement. "Just as soon as we're done rangering, me and the boys'll see there's a Cut Corners on the map."

Carolina nodded, and her satisfied look made him wish he believed the promise would come true as much as she seemed to. As far as he was concerned, however, he'd be a Texas Ranger until the day he died, and he knew the others felt the same way. Cut Corners would most likely stay a dream, but he would never admit that to Carolina.

"Second, make Christmas special for our Rafael. He and our Savior share a birthday, and I want you to make a grand celebration of the day, you hear?"

"Of course."

Now *that* he could do. He'd always been big on celebrating the Lord's birth. The only wrinkle in that plan would be figuring out how to get through the day without missing his Carolina. Eb shifted positions to lie beside her. If only he could stop the clock, take away time's ability to move forward.

"Lina," he said as he buried his face in her dark hair, "I love you."

His wife sighed. "No better husband ever drew a breath

than you, Eb Wilson. I do not ask this last thing of you out of spite but rather out of love. Do you understand?"

"Yes," he managed.

"Mi amour," she said as she peered at him, "our son must never ever be a Texas Ranger."

The hardest words Eb Wilson ever said were, "I promise."

The Marrying Kind

by Kathleen Y'Barbo

Dedication

To Meg Shaheen. . .for taking Hannah under your wing
and into your carpool so I could write on Thursday nights.
And to Evie for being a forever friend to Hannah.
May God bless you as much as you have blessed me.

And he said unto them, How is it that ye sought me?
Wist ye not that I must be about my Father's business?

LUKE 2:49

Prologue

Cut Corners, Texas
Christmas Day, 1871

S ure feels good to finally keep my promise, even if it did take nigh on twenty years. Guess it goes to show you can't rush the Lord. It all happens in His time, don't it?"

Eb Wilson sat atop his favorite horse and stared at the beginnings of the town called Cut Corners. None of them could remember which of the four former rangers had come up with the name, but they all agreed it fit the little spot on the north Texas prairie to a *T*.

Now, with a light dusting of snow, Main Street and its

collection of finished and partially finished buildings looked prettier than ever. From the train station to the little church where they would worship that morning, signs of progress abounded.

Tomorrow the work would continue, but this day, the Savior's birthday, was reserved for celebration. After church they would celebrate Rafe's birthday, too, just as Eb had done every year, keeping his promise to Carolina.

Carolina.

Eb swallowed hard and cast a glance skyward. *I miss you, mi amour. I only hope Rafe and I have made you proud.*

"Ja," Lars Olson, better known as Swede, said under his breath. "Cut Corners. Can you believe it is finally real?"

Eb cast a glance over his shoulder at his nephew, blacksmith Jeff Wilson, who drove the buckboard filled with gifts for the town's few children. Beside him, Rafe wore a grin.

The two of them were quite a pair, cousins and friends but raised like brothers. More often than not, they were partners in crime, as well, although their adult years and the fact that Rafe had agreed to act as sheriff of Cut Corners in the coming year had slowed their antics a bit.

"It's not done yet," Rafe said as he climbed out of the buckboard and helped his cousin secure the horse. "Won't be for a long time."

"That's the truth, Son. We still have a long way to go," Eb said, "but with hard work and prayer, it's going to be done before we know it. Then all we'll have to do is ask the Lord and our new sheriff to keep it safe."

From inside the little church building, a chorus of voices rose. Eb checked his watch. Straight up eleven, and time for services to begin. The new preacher sure was prompt.

"Onward then," Charles P. "Chaps" Smythe said as his boots hit the ground. "We have a church service to attend. I'd hate to think the four distinguished gentlemen who had the vision to found this town would be late to its first Christmas morning service."

"Are we late already?" Stone Creedon asked. "My watch must be slow."

"No, we're right on time," Eb said, being sure to speak into his slightly hard-of-hearing friend's good ear.

He let the young men walk ahead of the group, allowing them to disappear into the church building before he spoke. "Gentlemen, I'd like to thank you all." The lump in his throat almost kept him from finishing what he had to say. Almost but not quite. "There's not a one of us who can take more credit than the other for getting this town started up, but I feel like I'm the one you all did a favor for."

"How so?" Stone asked.

"Well, if it weren't for my Carolina, rest her soul, I'd probably have been content to dream about this place until the Lord took me home."

Chaps clapped a hand on Eb's back. "Sometimes a man needs a nudge to get going on what the Lord intends him to do. For you, your wife's passing was that nudge." He paused to look at the others before turning his attention back to Eb. "For the three of us, it was a friend and fellow ranger's promise."

"Ja, that's right," Swede said. "When you think of it, we are all fulfilling a promise to serve the Lord and the state of Texas."

"That we are," Stone said. "I say we dedicate this town to Him right here and now. What say you, fellow rangers?"

"I'm in on that." Eb held his hand out, and the others clasped theirs atop it. The four former rangers, comrades on the trail and friends in retirement, huddled together.

Rafe appeared at the church door. "Preacher's waiting," he said. "You can't miss the first Christmas service."

"Indeed. Shall we reconvene this meeting of the founding fathers at a later hour, say over dominoes after lunch tomorrow?"

"Who are you now, the mayor?" Swede asked Chaps with a grin.

"Actually I hadn't considered the office, but if you're offering it, then I'll heartily accept."

"After you, Stone, Swede, Mr. Mayor," Eb said with a sweep of his hat. "Save me a spot down front."

As the last of his fellow rangers filed past, Eb paused to once again look toward the sky. "Thank You, Lord," he said softly. "I do indeed dedicate this town and all that takes place here to Your glory. Keep those who live here safe from harm. And if You think about it, could You tell my wife, Carolina, that I love her and I sure do miss her?"

Chapter 1

Christmas Eve, 1877

It was Christmas Eve, and when I opened my mouth to sing, a hymn came out. Mama sent me to my room so the gentlemen callers wouldn't hear. No doubt the Lord wasn't as welcome as the other menfolk in Mama's parlor."

Peony Primrose Periwinkle Potter shifted positions and dabbed at the perspiration on her brow with her mama's best silk handkerchief, no doubt a gift from some hapless fool bent on taking Mama away from a life she had no intention of leaving. Despite the chilly winter temperatures outside, the tight confines of the railcar made the room feel more like summer.

The train's horn sounded, and Peony sighed. "No trifling with men for me. I plan to open a dress store, you know. A nice establishment with lace curtains and a pretty mirror for the ladies to see themselves in. I've been collecting scrap fabric ever since I was a little girl for just that purpose."

Peony peered over at her traveling companion, unsure as to why she'd just rattled on to him about the intimate details of her life as a New Orleans bawdy house owner's daughter. Perhaps it was because the sweet old man was stone-cold deaf and fast asleep.

Mr. Connor snored softly, his head gently bobbing with the rhythm of the train as it headed west. Peony smiled to think of how the Lord had arranged it so that she went out to fetch water at just the right time to overhear one of Mama's customers lament at having to take his valuable time to escort his elderly father out west.

"So I volunteered to see you safely to your destination, Mr. Connor. Mama didn't dare go against her best customer." Peony shrugged. "The way I see it, the Lord heard my prayer, and the rest is history."

She squared her shoulders and closed her eyes. As bad as her days with Mama had been, things could have turned out much worse. *Thank You, Lord, that Mama never wanted me to be one of her "girls."* Still, after seeing what she'd seen and living as she'd lived, Peony knew she might never be considered fit for decent folk.

All the more reason to start over somewhere new.

Visions of silks and satins danced across her mind, chased by silver thimbles and golden threads. Finally, her skill at hemming the dresses of Mama's girls and adding ruffles and flourishes to their lacy underthings would come in handy.

To think it all seemed so far from her grasp mere days ago. Next Christmas she'd celebrate her Savior's birthday in style—or at least in safety. Back home in New Orleans, Christmas had been just another day on Mama's busy social calendar. When Papa lived with them, it had been a day to gamble and play cards.

For a moment, Peony allowed her thoughts to wander toward memories of her beloved papa. She had vague recollections of a dark-haired man with a tickly beard who could lift her over his shoulders and toss her into the air with ease.

Later she knew this same man as a down-on-his-luck shadow of his former self, a man so broken by the weight of his habit that she could scarcely recognize him. Finally, somewhere around her fourth or fifth year, he'd disappeared entirely. That's when Mama began using the big house on Royal Street for something other than a home.

How she despised gambling in any form.

She settled back and watched the Texas landscape roll by until she could no longer hold her eyelids open. Somewhere between the purple fingers of dawn and the bright noonday sun, the train shuddered to a stop. Peony blinked hard and shook away the grogginess.

Placing a gloved hand atop her charge's blue-veined one, she stifled a yawn. Someday soon, she'd be sleeping in a real bed in a room with a door she didn't have to bar with a kitchen chair to keep Mama's clientele from "accidentally" trying to climb beneath her covers.

She shuddered with the memory, then purposefully turned her thoughts back to the elderly gentleman beside her. "The sign at the depot says we're in Dallas, Texas. It's a lovely day. Shall we take this opportunity to step outside, Mr. Connor?"

No response. Of course. He was fast asleep and couldn't hear her.

She shook his hand. "Mr. Connor?"

Nothing. Trying again, she got the same result. Despite her best efforts, the old man continued to sit head down, his chin resting on his narrow upper body.

Peony leaned closer and touched her palm to his chest. No response.

"Oh no," she whispered. "Mr. Connor, you're dead."

Muffled voices drew near, then passed by, oblivious to Peony's plight. She dabbed at her temples, her gaze darting from the open door to the open window. Which one offered the safer means of escape? The door beckoned but offered the added chance she might be spotted by someone while traversing the passageway. To slip out the open window seemed her only option.

Gathering her things, Peony prepared to make good on her escape. She swung her traveling bag onto her shoulder and put one foot on the bench. Using the window's frame for balance, she climbed up and prepared to slip out the window. The tracks were deserted in either direction, and the fall seemed to be one that she could survive. She'd walk away bruised, but at least she would walk away.

There would be nothing to connect her to the dead man. Nothing to hinder her from creating a new and respectable life.

The conductor called, "All aboard!" off in the distance as Peony leaned over the window's wooden frame and prepared to drop her bag onto the tracks. A pang of conscience hit her hard. What would happen to Mr. Connor?

One last look over her shoulder and Peony knew she couldn't just slip away and leave the kind old man to an unmarked grave on some Texas version of Boot Hill. She let the bag fall at her feet and climbed off the bench to retrieve a pen and writing paper from her reticule. Hurriedly scribbling a note for the conductor to find, she identified Mr. Connor's son by name and address, then wrote simply, "He died of natural causes, I promise."

"There, Mr. Connor," she whispered as she placed the note in his lapel pocket. "Now I'll know you're going to be taken care of."

She smoothed the fabric back into place, then paused. What was that? Reaching deeper into his pocket, past the note she'd just placed there, she found quite a surprise. Money. A fat wad of it, folded in half and secured with a red ribbon.

Peony counted the stack, then stifled a gasp. "Seven hundred dollars."

Carefully replacing the bills in the old man's pocket, she fell back against the hard wooden bench and closed her eyes. "Think," she whispered. "What do I do?"

The urge to run still bore hard on her. She tamped down her panic and allowed logic to take over. By the time the conductor arrived at the door, she had a plan—and seven hundred dollars in the waistband of her skirt.

It took her all of ten minutes to convince the authorities of her grief, scarcely longer than that to be driven to the undertaker in the sheriff's buggy to purchase a suitable casket and a plot in a nice cemetery atop a green hill near town. Declining the undertaker's offer to find lodging beneath his roof, Peony settled for a small room at a boardinghouse near the station. As darkness began to gather in the corners of the little room, Peony spread her remaining funds on the thread-bare bedspread.

Just over six hundred dollars remained after the day's carefully budgeted expenses. A fortune to her—nothing, she was certain, to the younger Mr. Connor.

Exhaustion tugged at her senses, and it was all Peony could do to slip the money back into her waistband and rise to head outside once more. She reached her destination in a few steps, the telegraph office being the only building stand-ing between the rooming house and the train station.

Obviously accustomed to discretion, the Western Union clerk barely blinked when Peony handed over three hundred and seventeen dollars and forty-three cents along with a note addressed to Robert Walker Livingston Connor III of New Orleans. She'd labored over the words, ultimately tell-ing the younger Mr. Connor where he could find his father and why. She gave a full accounting of the monies she spent buying a proper casket and burial plot. Finally, she added a note of condolence and a receipt for payment of three hun-dred dollars, exactly half the money she'd agreed to.

After all, she'd only accompanied him halfway.

Half an hour later, she returned to her room and fell atop the narrow bed, not bothering to remove her traveling clothes. She would need them soon enough.

Chapter 2

Christmas Day, 1877

Rafe Wilson stepped away from his birthday celebration to cast a glance out the back window of Millie's Diner. Pop and his three constant companions raced across the broad expanse of space to slip behind the privy.

He chuckled. Like as not, the four of them were plotting trouble. Well, they'd earned the right.

Together the men formed the backbone of a ranger unit that, in its heyday, struck fear in the hearts of outlaws from San Antonio to the Brazos River and on up to the Oklahoma border.

Slowed by age, the four had lost none of their ranger camaraderie. They had, since entering retirement, shifted their focus from clearing Texas soil of evildoers to arguing the finer points of nearly everything while presiding over the town of Cut Corners. For the past seven years, the quartet and their various friends and acquaintances had turned their little place on the Texas prairie into a right fine home for God-fearing folk.

If he weren't so anxious to leave, he'd be glad to call the place home. Why, it would be a nice place to set up housekeeping with a pretty girl, maybe raise up a passel of young'uns.

Too bad he wasn't the marrying kind.

❧

"I don't care what the captain says. Rafe's not joining up with the rangers, and that's that."

"He's a full-grown man, Eb. Older than you were when you took the oath," Swede said. "I don't see how you can stop him if he takes a notion to go."

"Don't worry. I've got a plan."

Eb leaned away from his hiding place behind the privy and checked to see if the coast was clear. Thus far, no one inside Millie's Diner had noticed the absence of the town's four original citizens. From the laughter drifting toward them, the dual celebration of Christmas and Rafe's birthday was still going strong.

Soon Millie would insist Rafe make a birthday wish and take the first slice of cake. That's where the party usually went south. While everyone in Cut Corners loved Millie, her cooking left something to be desired. Too bad she put all the sugar in the pot roast and none of it into her birthday cakes. Even though her pound cake could pound nails, Millie had practically raised Rafe and his cousin Jeff, too. Leaving her out of the family party that always followed the Christmas service at church never entered Eb's mind.

Setting her kitchen afire so she couldn't offer up her grub at the festivities—now that had occurred to him on more than one occasion. Too bad he was a law-abiding citizen and a God-fearing man.

"You've always got some sort of plan, Eb." Chaps jabbed his ribs with a sharp elbow. "I hope this one's better than the time you set the hogs on the preacher's garden. I thought we never would catch those critters once Rafe scattered them with buckshot."

"Well, it worked, didn't it? Before he lit out after those hogs, my son had about as much interest in his sheriffing as he did in learning to knit purty. Ever since then, he's been walking with a spring in his step and acting like he's useful around here." He paused. "Until lately, that is."

"Late?" Stone, deaf as a doorpost in one ear, turned to walk away. "We don't want to be late. We might miss the birthday singin'. The cake, now that's another story."

Eb caught his friend's elbow and spun him around. "We're not late yet," he said into the man's good ear.

"Well, why didn't you say so?" Stone grumbled. "I don't want to be late lessen it's for the cake eatin'."

"So you really think your harebrained scheme will work?" Swede asked. "Maybe we should just have a talk with the boy, explain to him that his mama didn't want him to be a ranger, and leave it at that. That makes sense, ja?"

Eb had pondered that possibility for years. Setting the boy straight on his mama's bias against rangering seemed like a tempting prospect, one that would certainly get him off the hook. While the finer points of the plan were obvious, Eb never could get past the idea that somehow the knowledge that his mama went to her reward with a dislike for the rangers might make Rafe think less of her. One thing Eb Wilson would never do was tarnish the memory of his beloved Carolina.

No, he had to keep his peace about the promise he made to her. The Lord and his ranger friends would have to help him out on this one.

"Trust me," Eb said. "This plan's foolproof."

Chaps leaned back against the rough wall of the privy and peered up at Eb from beneath the brim of his bowler hat. "That's what I'm worried about, my friend."

"What do you mean?" Eb narrowed his eyes. "Don't you want Rafe to stay in Cut Corners?"

"Of course I do," the Englishman said. "But I am a bit concerned about being shot in the process. If you'll recall, he didn't miss when he aimed at the pigs."

"Yes, I do recall that. Who do you think taught the boy how to shoot?"

"Millie, actually," Chaps said. "So what's your point?"

Eb ignored his friend's joke and offered a knowing smile. "The point is that even though Captain Phelps keeps me posted on things, I can't help but wonder when Rafe's going to come around to talking to him about joining up. You know he's taken quite an interest in my boy."

"Phelps is a good man," Chaps said, "but if Rafe decides to join up, there's not much he can do. Your boy's a born ranger, and any company would be lucky to get him. If Phelps won't take him, one of the other company commanders will."

Swede nodded. "Ja, I see how that might cause you to worry about your promise to Carolina, but the boy's a man now. How can we interfere?"

"Well, we won't exactly be interfering," Eb said. "I like to think of it as helping the Lord along with His plan."

"Sounds like meddlin' to me," Stone said.

Eb narrowed his eyes and stared at each of his friends in turn. "Well then, any of you fellows object to being called meddlin' men?"

"Nope," Stone said.

Chaps smiled. "Not I."

"What about you, Swede? You mind being a meddler?"

"In this instance, I don't mind."

"Well then, it's settled." He hit the high points of a strategy so brilliant he couldn't believe he'd thought of it. "Now, the thing is, until we know for sure that he's making plans to sign up with the rangers, we just keep the scheme on the back burner. Deal?"

Stone shook his head. "Burning? Somebody say something's burning? That Millie must of done gone and set the kitchen afire." He chuckled and slapped Eb hard on the back. "That there's an answer to prayer."

"No, my friend," Chaps shouted. "The kitchen's fine."

The former ranger looked about as happy as a long-tailed cat in a room full of rocking chairs. "Well now, that's too bad."

"Eb Wilson, are you and those friends of yours out

there? You better get in here afore Christmas and your only boy's twenty-sixth birthday is done over and gone."

"Uh-oh, it's Millie." Eb paused and looked at his friends. "Look, are we agreed on this? We wait until the time's right, then we implement the plan. In the meantime, we pray Rafe doesn't get some wild idea and take off for San Antonio and the rangers."

⁂

Daylight sliced across Peony's sore eyes. Something jabbed her in the ribs, and with care, she leaned away from the offending spring to reach for the edge of the mattress. Where was she? Shaking off the cobwebs of last night's disturbing dream, she placed her feet on the floor, fully expecting to feel the rocking of the rails beneath her and hear the roar of a train's engine. Instead, she heard a loud rap at the door.

"Management," a female voice called. "It's high noon and past time to go."

Gathering her wits, she stumbled toward the door and threw it open. A rather surly-looking woman of advanced years stood inches away.

"Noon?" she said as she stifled a yawn. "Already?"

"Yes'm, it's nigh on half past, actually, and ya gotta vacate, hon," the woman said. "Room's been rented." She took a step back and gestured toward the stairs with her thumb. "That'un there paid me for a whole month. I'll hold him off a minute or two so's you can change."

An older fellow, spry but graying, headed their way at a fast clip. Peony looked down at the wrinkled mess she'd made of her only traveling dress. Although she looked a fright, there was no one in Dallas she needed to pretty up for.

"No, really," she said as she stepped away from the door. "Let me just fetch my bag and I'll be out of your way. I meant to be on my way to the train station hours ago."

"Ain't no train till late this afternoon," the older woman said. "Like as not you'll find the benches hard down at the station. 'Sides, it's Christmas. Nobody's gonna be keeping to a schedule today."

Christmas. Peony's heart sank. She'd all but forgotten. Back home, the bells on the cathedral would be ringing out the good news of the Christ-Child's birth. At Mama's place, however, it would most likely be business as usual.

"Where you headed, anyway?"

"West. North. I haven't exactly decided, although I've prayed about it quite a lot." She shrugged. "Anywhere a good seamstress is needed and reasonably priced storefront space can be had."

"Now isn't that interesting?"

Peony whirled around to see the elderly gentleman

35

standing in the doorway. He held a battered hat in his hand and carried a valise under his arm. His linen suit belied the fact that Dallas had awakened to the coldest day in the month of December so far.

"Thomas Holcombe," he said with a smart nod. "Pleased to make your acquaintance."

She returned the greeting, then offered a weak smile.

Mr. Holcombe gave her a quick shake of his head, then addressed the proprietor of the hotel. "I'll not be responsible for putting this gentlewoman out on the street on Christmas Day." Dropping his valise at his side, he crossed his arms over his chest. "I insist she be allowed to stay. I will remain in the dining room until the lady can secure a ticket and be escorted to the train. If she cannot make arrangements until tomorrow, then so be it. I'll take lodging elsewhere."

The woman snorted. "Only empty rooms in Dallas on Christmas Day's at the jailhouse, and that ain't for certain."

"No, really, I insist." Peony stuffed her feet into her shoes and slipped the handle of her bag onto the crook of her arm. "I've missed breakfast, and I'm about to miss lunch, too." She slipped past the linen-clad man to address the proprietor. "Would it be improper for a single woman to sit alone in your dining room?"

The older woman gave a most unladylike snort. "Hon,

this is Dallas. You come on downstairs with me, and I'll see you're not bothered."

A few moments later, Peony found herself settled at a corner table near the kitchen and under the watchful eyes of the proprietor's son, an overlarge man of middle years. While her stomach offered the dual complaints of hunger and queasiness, her heart offered only one—desperation. She closed her eyes and offered a blessing over the plate of home-cooked fare, finishing with a plea more centered on her future than on the meal presently before her.

Lord, You led me out here—I just know it. Why have You left me high and dry in Dallas, Texas, on the very day Your Son was born? This was supposed to be my best Christmas ever. Now what do I do, Lord?

Chapter 3

The sound of a man clearing his throat broke into her prayer. Peony opened her eyes to see Mr. Holcombe standing before her.

"I'm very glad to see you're still here," he said. "I feel just terrible putting you out of your room, especially with it being a holiday and all."

She waved away his concern with a sweep of her hand. "Think nothing of it, sir. I assure you I'll be heading for. . ." Peony paused. She peered up at the gentleman, who now stared at her expectantly. "Well, I'll be heading out of Dallas very soon."

Touching the corners of her lips with the rough napkin, Peony hid her frown. Perhaps the man would leave if she acted disinterested. She stabbed at a salted hothouse tomato slice and took a bite. He stood watching her chew until she swallowed both the tomato and her fears and asked him to join her.

Peony gave the dapper Mr. Holcombe a sideways look, smiling despite herself as he winked and said, "I assure you I'm far too old for anything other than dinner. I'm nothing but an old reporter looking to change my ways. I'm working on a book, you know."

"A book?" She set her fork down and narrowed her eyes. The wrong answer would send her scurrying for the train station for sure. "What's your book about, sir?"

He shrugged and rested his elbows on the gently worn checked tablecloth. "My adventures," he said. "All those years chronicling the ways of Texas seem to be paying off. I'm actually being paid a livable wage this time, to boot."

"But don't you have family you'd rather spend time with today?"

His answer lay in the expression on his face.

"Oh, I'm terribly sorry. I shouldn't have asked," Peony said.

"Actually I don't mind the question. It's the answer that's difficult." The reporter offered a weak smile. "You see, I was once a family man with a wife almost as pretty as you."

"What happened?" The question was out before she could take it back. She winced. "I'm sorry. Again I've overstepped the bounds of propriety."

"Nonsense," he said. "The nomadic life of a reporter didn't set well with my bride. She took our little girl and went home to her mama some years back."

"You simply have to go to them." Once more she'd spoken before her good sense could stop her. "Forgive me. Perhaps I'm speaking out of turn because it's Christmas Day and I'm here in this place without a family of my own. It's just that I know—or rather, I can imagine—that it would be most difficult for a girl to grow up without her father."

Mr. Holcombe's face grew solemn, and he seemed to give great thought to her words. The pain of the memory of growing up without her own father burned almost as bright as the shame of thinking she might have accidentally told someone about it.

"Just consider it," she said quickly. "Think about making things right with your family."

A smile lit the older man's face. "If I didn't know better, I'd think you were some sort of Christmas angel sent to guide me home."

Peony laughed out loud at the thought of her being any sort of angel. "I don't know that the Lord has any use for the likes of me, but if I've given you something to think about, I'm grateful to Him for providing the words."

"Well, you have." He paused. "So, why don't you tell me more about what brings you to this worthy establishment on Christmas Day?"

Peony winced. "I'd much rather you tell me your story than to bore you with mine."

Moments later, the gentleman was entertaining Peony with tales of his two decades of newspapering, the most recent centering on a place called Cut Corners, Texas.

Somewhere along the way, Peony managed to finish her lunch and two of the best cups of coffee she'd had all week. She also confided her hopes for a future designing dresses, making him the second stranger in as many days with whom she'd shared her carefully guarded dreams.

By the time Mr. Holcombe pulled a gold pocket watch from his lapel, she'd all but forgotten she had no plans beyond lunch save the short walk to the train station. She hadn't considered whether the train would be heading east or west, and she told him so when he asked.

"Perhaps I can provide an impetus to set you aboard a train going north."

"North?" She placed the folded napkin beside her coffee cup and topped it with a few coins.

He looked away and seemed to be considering whether to speak. Finally, his gaze met hers. "My dear, I do believe the town of Cut Corners is in dire need of a dressmaker." He leaned forward. "And I am in dire need of someone to purchase a certain empty newspaper office set right on the main thoroughfare."

Peony gathered her traveling bag into her lap. The most she could spare would be a meager one hundred dollars, a sum so low she dare not mention it for fear of offending the kind man.

"I'm sorry, Mr. Holcombe, I don't have the money to—"

"You'd be doing me a great favor." He waved away her protest, then removed a slip of folded paper from his linen jacket and set it on the tabletop between them. With gnarled hands, Mr. Holcombe smoothed out the document, a deed, and turned it toward Peony. "Could you afford one hundred dollars?"

❧

Ten months later, on the last day of October, Peony stepped out of the train station and stopped at the edge of the platform, taking a moment to look over the peaceful little town of Cut Corners, Texas. Not much to it, just as Mr. Holcombe had warned, but still it fairly resembled the image she carried in her mind. She reached into the pocket of her traveling dress and pulled out the key to her future.

Giggling at the pun, she set off toward Main Street and the old newspaper office, soon to be the home of her new dressmaking shop. The first of several trunks of essentials was due to arrive from Dallas in a few days, so until then, she would have to make do with what she'd managed to fit into the carpetbag at her side.

And make do, she would. After working as a maid at the boardinghouse in Dallas since the day after Christmas, she'd finally scrimped and saved enough to purchase a proper inventory for her dressmaker's shop. She'd even managed to purchase a used Singer sewing machine.

Offering a smile to the dapper man at the telegraph office, she marched across Ranger Road onto Main and strolled along until she stood in front of the building—her building—situated between a boardinghouse and a diner with a hand-lettered sign reading MILLIE'S DINER. A stiff north breeze kicked up the hem of her skirt and blew a strand of hair into her eyes as she fitted the key into the lock.

"Thank You, Lord," she whispered. "Without Your intervention, none of this would be possible." Adding a promise to dedicate all she did to God, Peony threw open the door and stepped into her—

She froze.

The place was a mess. Dark streaks decorated one wall, and the residue of printer ink hung heavy in the air.

Against her better judgment, she stepped over the threshold into her new life, a life so far removed from New Orleans that it made her smile despite the mess surrounding her. Setting her carpetbag beside the door, she knelt right there and again thanked the Lord for bringing her to Cut Corners.

"Well, I declare. Looks like I've got me a churchgoin' woman for a neighbor."

Peony stumbled to her feet and swiped at the mess she'd made of her already dusty traveling skirt. A woman of fiftysomething stood in the doorway, her iron gray hair pulled off her face and captured in a messy knot atop her head.

Shaking the older woman's outstretched hand, Peony offered a smile and a soft "Yes, ma'am."

"Well now, that is an answer to prayer." She placed her hands on her hips and shook her head. "Old Man Holcombe hasn't gone on to the Lord, has he?"

"Mr. Holcombe? Oh no. He's fine. I last saw him in Dallas. He is working on a book about his travels in Texas."

"Is that right?" A broad grin split her lined face. "Well, you don't look much like your daddy, but I sure am glad he finally found you." Confusion must have etched Peony's face, for the woman gave her a sideways look. "You are Tom

Holcombe's long-lost daughter, aren't you?"

"No, ma'am," she said. "He's still looking for her."

The woman made a clucking sound. "A pity, that situation. I told him he oughtn't to stop until he finds that girl and her mama."

"I told him the same thing." Silence fell between them, punctuated by the shrill call of the train's whistle. Funny how just moments ago she had been on that train, and now here she stood in her store with her neighbor.

Back in New Orleans the decent folk they had for neighbors didn't speak to Peony or her mama. At least not in public.

"Goodness, where are my manners? I'm Millie from next door. I run the diner. Nice to meet ya."

"I'm Peony. Peony Potter." She cringed when she said the name aloud, as she always did. Why Mama hadn't named her something sensible like Mary or Jane, she would never know. If she ever had daughters of her own, they certainly wouldn't be strapped with a moniker as silly as Peony Primrose Periwinkle Potter.

"Where you from, Miss Potter?"

"New—" She clamped her lips tight. Better not to give even a hint of her background. "I just arrived on the train from Dallas," she said. "And please, call me Peony."

Chapter 4

"Y"ou aim to open up another newspaper?"

Peony breathed a sigh of relief that Millie hadn't seemed to give her unusual name or her faltering explanation of her hometown a second thought—or perhaps she thought it rude to comment. She and the older woman would be fast friends if this was any indication of Millie's character.

"No," she said. "My intention is to open a dressmaker's shop. I sew, you see."

"Well now, isn't that nice?" She looked past Peony to the room beyond. "Looks like you've got a job ahead of you."

Nodding, Peony turned to follow Millie's gaze. "Yes, well, I wasn't expecting something so. . .so, well. . .in need of a woman's touch."

Millie cackled with laughter. "That it does," she said. "Actually, I'm thinking it might need some male attention first."

"How so?"

The older woman pointed to the jumble of tables and shelves stacked at the back of the room. "That there used to be where old Tom would put together his paper. If'n you take that big old board down, you'll find a right nice window. And those shelves, well, wouldn't they look nice up here in front with your goods stacked on them all purty?"

Peony pictured the changes in her mind. "Yes," she said. "That sounds wonderful. Perhaps you might know someone with some carpentering skills."

Her guest frowned and crossed her arms over her chest. "You don't have a husband to help you? A purty young thing like you?"

"No, ma'am," she said.

"You a widow already?"

"No, ma'am. I've never been married."

"Well, isn't that something." Millie took a step back to stare at Peony. "Looks like you haven't seen a full plate in a coon's age. Why, I bet I've got something simmering on the stove that'd put some meat on your bones. Why don't we step next door and I'll fix you a bite to eat? Then we can talk about how you're going to get this little place shining like a new penny."

A good meal would be a welcome distraction and a nice beginning to her new life in Cut Corners. "Thank you," Peony said as she shouldered her carpetbag. "I'd like that very much."

"Set your suitcase down, honey," Millie said. "Ain't nobody going to mess with it. You're in Cut Corners now. We don't have any crime. Sheriff Wilson sees to that."

"What does Sheriff Wilson see to?"

Peony looked past her new neighbor to see her doorway filled with a dark-haired man. His uniform told her he was the law in Cut Corners, but his demeanor and slow Texas drawl told her he'd seen his fill of silly women like her. At least that was the impression she got as she felt his gaze sweep past her to focus on Millie.

A lady would have been offended. Unfortunately, she was still learning how to be a lady.

While she waited for the outrage she knew she should feel, she studied the breadth of his shoulders and the deep dimple in his clean-shaven chin. By the time she focused her attention on his velvet brown eyes, she knew this was a man who could pose a serious threat. Not only was he the law in Cut Corners, and thus a man in a position to find out much more than she wanted him to know about her past, but he was also a thief.

One look at him and he'd stolen her breath. What would five minutes in his presence do?

Perhaps she should leave now, walk out of Cut Corners with her finances in ruins but her heart still intact. She'd only had to hear Mama's story of lost love, desperate circumstances, and wrong choices once to know that retreat was often the best option.

Luggage still in hand, she should march right back to the depot and forget she'd ever seen eyes so brown and hair so blue-black. If the Lord got her out of New Orleans, then getting her out of Cut Corner, Texas, would be simple.

Getting that dimple out of her mind, well, that would probably take a bit longer.

What am I thinking?

Peony clutched the carpetbag to her chest and stared at the ink-streaked floorboards beneath her feet. This was her dream, her destiny. Whatever this silly feeling of butterflies in her stomach meant, it surely wasn't going to keep her from what the Lord intended for her to do.

No, she would not take off running like a scalded cat just because some man turned her mind to mush and set her heart beating double time. Unlike Mama, she planned to set down roots and live a respectable life earning a respectable living without turning the fool over a man.

Peony squared her shoulders and stared head-on into the face of the man she would have to begin thinking of as the enemy—the enemy of her heart, anyway. She'd already sunk her savings into this little piece of Cut Corners; she had nowhere else to go. All she had to do was learn to avoid Sheriff Wilson at all costs, and she would be fine.

"Well now," Millie said. "You see what I mean. Speak of the law, and there he is. Come here, Rafe Wilson, and meet Miss Potter." She turned to Peony. "Miss Potter, this here is Sheriff Rafael Wilson. He's in charge of keeping the peace in Cut Corners."

"Ma'am." Rafe tipped his hat to the piece of fluff, then returned his attention to Millie, who'd obviously just paused to take a breath. Uh-oh. She looked like she'd caught hold of an idea and was just about to let loose with it. *Probably ought to head back where I came from.* He knew from experience that when Millie chewed on something, she stayed at it awhile.

"Miss Potter's gone and bought this building from Tom Holcombe. She's gonna make a dress shop out of this place. Aren't you, hon?"

The woman smiled and nodded but said nothing. Interesting. A female who didn't rattle on. And a pretty one, at that.

"Rafe here's been the sheriff for, well, how long's it been?"

He jabbed his fists into his pockets and forced a smile. "Nigh on to seven years now."

"Seven years," Millie repeated. "My how time does fly."

Seven years of presiding over a town where the most exciting thing that happened was the occasional drunk rolling out of the saloon to shoot up a couple of windows or a pig getting stuck in a well. While other sheriffs were dealing with Indian uprisings or outlaws, all Rafe Wilson had to worry about was whether the loose nail in his chair was going to poke his backside during his afternoon nap.

Millie's giggle drew his attention away from the new dressmaker. The older woman shrugged. "Has it been that long? Seems like yesterday we were holding church up the street for the first time and thanking the Lord we didn't have to live in tents anymore."

Millie stopped her jawing and took a step back, crossing her arms over her chest. For a second she studied the both of them, and then she grinned.

Something was up, and Rafe already knew he didn't like it. Time to make his escape.

He thrust his hand in the dressmaker's direction in an attempt to make good on his exit. She lifted her gaze. It collided with his, and he felt the jolt down to his toes. At that moment, something inside him shifted, and his heart did a big old flip-flop while his throat froze up tighter than a puddle of milk at the North Pole.

He couldn't be sure what it was or why it happened, but Rafe knew that trouble was brewing. What sort of trouble remained to be seen, but he felt confident it had everything to do with the new dressmaker.

A chorus of male voices tumbled toward them on the east wind. The object of his thoughts raised her pretty brows, then turned her pink lips into a frown. Dropping her carpetbag, Miss Potter moved toward him.

Rafe scooted out of the way just as she brushed past to step out onto the boardwalk. She smelled pretty, this little lady, and it was all he could do not to inhale deep one more time after she'd passed by. Instead, he followed her outside like a pup on a rope. When she stopped, so did he.

"What are they doing?" she asked in an agitated tone.

"Hmm, what?" He followed the direction she pointed.

A few feet away Pop and his ranger friends had set their pickle barrel and board contraption up in a small sliver of sunshine. Stone and Chaps were busy setting up the domino game. Pop and Swede stood nearby jawing about whose turn it was to cut firewood for the church stove Sunday morning.

"Looks like a regular Tuesday morning in Cut Corners, ma'am."

"Gambling and wayward men? Is that what this town supports? Well, I never."

Pop caught sight of him and waved, and Rafe returned the gesture. "Wayward men? Those four? Hardly."

Rafe smiled down at the feisty female, hoping to either rile her further or placate her. Both options promised to offer an entertaining result.

What was left of his good humor began to fade as all four former rangers turned to stare in his direction. Pop said something to Stone, who needled Chaps. All four roared with laughter.

"Great," Rafe said under his breath. By supper the whole town would know he'd paid a visit to the new dressmaker. Pop would ride him about it for ages. So would Jeff.

"Aren't you going to do something about them?"

Rafe forced his attention back on Miss Potter. His heart still went *ker-thunk* when he looked at her, but his brain had the good sense to remind him womenfolk were nothing but trouble to a man with one foot on the train to San Antonio and ranger headquarters.

Rather than get all riled up, he shrugged. "Like as not someone will complain about someone else taking too long to make a move, and the four of them will end up at Millie's before noon. Most days that's how it happens."

The woman crossed her arms over her chest and gave him a look of disgust. "Surely you don't expect decent folk to be exposed to the likes of those—those. . .criminals." Squaring her shoulders, Miss Potter leaned toward him. "You're the sheriff. Do something." She turned up her pretty nose as the word left her lips.

The minute he laughed, Rafe knew he shouldn't have.

Chapter 5

With not so much as a how-do-you-do, the little dressmaker whirled around and headed inside, passing him with such force that his hat went flying.

"Hold on there," Rafe called. "What do you expect me to do?"

The woman practically skidded to a stop, then whirled around to stalk back toward him. Stopping inches away from his nose, she rose to her tiptoes and regarded him through narrowed eyes. "Sir, as the law in this town, you are expected to make the streets safe." Rafe cast a lazy glance to the left and then to the right. "Well, Miss Potter, maybe you'd know better than me, but I believe the streets look just fine. Course we've only got two of them here."

For a minute, she looked like she might speak. Rafe started thinking of what he'd say in response. Should he point out that the very criminals she was worried about were the same men who'd kept this part of the prairie safe for the better part of three decades? Maybe he ought to tell her real plain that if she didn't like the daily domino game in front of her establishment, she ought to pick another place to set up shop.

Before he could say a word, she turned on her heels and stormed away.

Out of the corner of his eye, he saw Millie smile. "What?" he asked as he grabbed his hat off the boardwalk.

"She's right. You ought to do something."

He watched the swirl of blue skirts swish around the corner and disappear into the back room. "You know as well as I do that there's nothing to be done with the likes of those four."

"I wasn't talking about your daddy and his ranger friends." Millie nudged Rafe, then shook her head and pointed inside the shop. "You really ought to go on in there and do something about her. She's liable to hurt herself."

A crash sounded somewhere in the depths of the future dress shop. Rafe took a step back from the door and whistled under his breath. "Miss Millie, I've never backed down from man or beast, but I believe I'm going to walk away from this fight before I find myself bested."

Tipping his hat, he turned to head for Erik's workshop. If his friend wouldn't take him on as a part-time employee, maybe he'd turn him loose with a hammer and bag of nails and let him pound away his riled-up temper on the scrap wood out back.

Another crash and Millie went skittering toward the diner like a scalded cat. Rafe was tempted to go back and make sure Miss Potter hadn't buried herself under an avalanche of old newspapers or fallen through the staircase that led up to the storeroom.

He stopped and waited. The only sound he heard was the cackle of Pop and the men laughing. Then the laughter stopped.

Rafe watched in disbelief as the town's new dressmaker appeared in her doorway wielding something that looked like a large stick. No, he decided, it was a broom she held.

"Gentlemen, I am going to ask you nicely to leave the premises immediately and take your gaming apparatus with you. I intend my dress shop to be a decent establishment, and I will not have my customers see such goings-on at my doorstep."

To her credit, she spoke nicely, but her face and the way she held that broom told another story. The little lady looked capable of breaking up the domino game by force at the slightest provocation.

Rafe leaned against the hitching post to watch the show. "This just could be the most fun I've had all day."

Chaps rose first and gave Miss Potter a courtly bow. No doubt back in England, he'd charmed his share of the ladies. The dressmaker, however, seemed oblivious.

"My friends," Chaps said as he collected the dominos, "I do believe it is time to reconvene this meeting of the town council elsewhere as the lady has requested."

"Yes, sir, Mr. Mayor." Pops lifted the board off the pickle barrel, then offered Miss Potter a smile. "Welcome to Cut Corners, ma'am. You sure do pretty up the place."

Rafe knew for a fact that Pop had done his share of lady charming in his day. Once again, the lady in question was not amused, however. Rafe chuckled at the sour face she made.

"Might I suggest though," Pop added, "that you take to carrying a pretty little reticule or a parasol of some sort? It's not that you don't look fetching holding it over your head like that, but something a little less threatening than a broom might better impress the menfolk."

"I give her a week and she'll be on the train out of town," Rafe said under his breath.

Stone gathered up the remaining stools while Chaps hefted the pickle barrel onto his shoulder. "Onward, men," he said as he led his band of brothers across Main Street.

"Don't forget it's my turn," Swede called.

She must have seen him laughing, for the dressmaker started his way. Rafe rose to his full height and squared his shoulders. He adjusted his holster, then fiddled with his badge to be sure it glittered just right in the morning sun.

A glance in her direction told him she'd neither slowed her pace nor dropped her broom. Rafe frowned. Surely she didn't intend to sweep the boardwalk with the sheriff of Cut Corners.

Not in broad daylight on Main Street.

"Sheriff Wilson?"

He met her halfway, then tipped his hat and looked down his nose at the prettiest sight that ever decorated the middle of Main Street. Her eyes were blue-green. Now how about that? He'd have sworn they were blue. And here in the sun her hair had the prettiest shades of honey mixed in with the brown. Her lips, now they were still pretty and pink just like he'd noticed back in the—

"Sheriff Wilson."

Rafe shook his head to clear his thoughts. "Yes, ma'am."

"Sir, you are the law in this town. Am I correct?"

He stared at the broom instead of the woman to keep his brain from running off and leaving him again. "You are."

"And you work for the law-abiding citizens of Cut Corners?"

"I do."

There he went looking at those eyes again. Rafe stared past her to the boardinghouse where Lula stood on the porch jawing with Ticks McGee. When Lula lifted her hand to wave, he responded with a nod.

Then he noticed the crowd gathering at the windows of Millie's place. It looked like half the town was watching them instead of eating. Of course, it was pot roast day, and that alone could have kept the diners from raising their forks.

She shook her broom and narrowed her eyes. My but she still looked pretty, even riled up like a banty rooster.

"Then, as a citizen of Cut Corners, I demand you end the lawlessness that seems to pervade this town."

Rafe watched the crowd gathering on the boardwalk outside Jay Harris's barbershop and frowned. Something had to be done about this menace to his peace and quiet.

"Do tell," was all he could manage.

"Indeed. You are needed, Sheriff. What will you do about it?"

A nagging voice reminded him that just this morning he'd prayed for the Lord to do something about the fact that he never seemed to be needed by the citizens of Cut Corners. When he uttered that prayer, he'd thought he was asking God to give him clear rein to join up with the rangers.

Now he had to wonder if the Heavenly Father didn't have a sense of humor.

"Well, ma'am, a man doesn't go into a fight unarmed, if you know what I mean." She obviously didn't, but he pressed on anyway. "So what I'm going to do is go back to my office and think on this. I'm going to get me a plan. How about that?"

She seemed to be chewing on the idea of complaining further. Finally she nodded. "I think that's a good idea."

"Well, praise the Lord. Now if you'll excuse me."

With that he turned tail and headed for the quiet confines of his office and the nap he planned to take just as soon as he calmed down. This afternoon he'd go see Erik. If the carpenter wouldn't take him on for free, he'd just have to pay Erik to work there.

The extra work ought to keep him busy and out of reach of the dressmaker's complaints. It would also serve to make the time pass quickly until he could make a trip to San Antonio.

If Peony Potter was putting down stakes in Cut Corners, it was time for him to pull his up.

Chapter 6

The first day of November dawned bright and clear, but Peony's eyes were anything but. She'd spent half the evening and into the night clearing out reams of old paper and scrubbing down windows and walls. Today she planned to tackle the ink-streaked floor and the dusty shelves. By the time her supplies arrived from Dallas, her shop would shine like a new penny.

Peony sipped gingerly from the steaming cup of coffee and gave thanks that Lula Chamberlain, owner of the boardinghouse that had become her temporary home, made the best around.

"Miss Potter, might I join you?" A man of considerable stature stood beside the empty chair. "I'm Thaddeus Seymour.

I'm the banker in these parts."

She nodded, and the fellow sank onto the chair. "Welcome to Cut Corners, Miss Potter."

"Thank you," she replied.

Rafe Wilson stepped into view, and her heart jumped. What a handsome man. A pity he was such a grump.

"As I was saying, your monies are more than safe in our little bank. Why just yesterday I was speaking to a fellow banker on the train back from Dallas, and he said. . ."

The fellow's mouth kept moving, but Peony heard none of what he said. Instead, she watched the sheriff pour a cup of coffee and disappear into the kitchen. A few seconds later, she heard the unmistakable laughter of Lula Chamberlain followed by a deep rumble that could only belong to Sheriff Wilson.

"Miss Potter?"

Peony tore her attention away from the kitchen door and focused on her companion. "Yes, I'm sorry. What were you saying?"

Mr. Seymour let out a long breath and smiled. "I was explaining how our system of compounding your interest. . ."

Interest. Yes, that's what she felt, but not in anything the banker said. More than anything else, she was interested in what was so funny behind the kitchen door. Twice now she'd heard the sheriff's laughter and, more than that, a giggle from Lula Chamberlain.

Why, the woman was old enough to be that man's mother. Surely the pair weren't, well, a pair.

The objects of her thoughts spilled through the door with the sheriff in the lead. He stopped short when his gaze met Peony's, causing Lula to run into him. His glass of milk went flying, and so did the pan of biscuits Lula held. The end result was a mess that landed partly on the floor and mostly on the banker.

Mr. Seymour clambered to his feet, howling at the indignity of cold milk trickling down his back and decorating his expensive suit. Lula rushed to placate the banker while Rafe winked at Peony. "Looks like we're both out of luck for breakfast," he said.

Peony nodded, stomach growling. With the biscuits a total ruin, the only alternative was the fare at Millie's place. If only she'd saved some of the jerky she'd purchased for her trip from Dallas. Unfortunately she'd eaten the last of it yesterday evening. At the time, it had seemed sensible to continue her work without leaving to dine at the boarding-house.

"Miss Potter, are you as hungry as I am?"

Peony jumped and clutched her napkin to her chest. For

a large man, Sheriff Wilson certainly could move quietly. Of course, the banker's howling would have drowned out all but the most careless of patrons.

Meeting his gaze, Peony noted the lawman had a glorious smile. "Actually I'm famished. Perhaps you could tell me whether Millie is still serving breakfast."

"Yes, she's still got breakfast cooking, but I have to warn you, good food's as scarce as hens' teeth over at Millie's place." The sheriff cringed. "I love her like my own mother, but what that woman does to biscuits ought to be illegal."

Peony giggled. "I did find yesterday's lunch quite interesting."

"Ah, the Monday lunch special. Pork chops and apple dumplings."

She nodded. "Funny, but I never knew a cook to put molasses in pork chops."

"And onions in the apple dumplings?"

"Exactly."

Rafe sighed. "Like I said, Millie's got a special place in my heart. It's her food I can't stomach. Pardon the pun." Silence fell between them, broken only by the thud of the banker's retreating footsteps and Lula's chuckle as she headed off to the kitchen, promising more biscuits in half an hour.

"Half an hour's a long time," Rafe said. "How about I

make up for ruining your breakfast by offering you a little something I've got over at my office? I keep a supply of jerky for emergencies." He gave her a sheepish look. "I couldn't help notice you like jerky."

"How would you know that?"

"Well, you see, I happened to be strolling past your shop last evening around sundown and noticed you having a picnic amongst the rubble." He looked pained at the admission. "I wasn't spying. I'd actually thought I might. . ."

"Might what?"

The sheriff frowned. "Well, now, I thought I might apologize for my rude behavior yesterday. See, I'm the law in Cut Corners, and as a citizen, you had every right to complain about the goings-on on your boardwalk. I guess I didn't do a very good job of explaining things."

"Explaining things?" She gave him a sideways look. "What things?"

Warning bells went off in Rafe's brain as the words he spoke hung in the silence. He'd been smoothing out her ruffled feathers with his sweet talk, and now this? With one sentence he'd set their relationship back to square one.

Not that they had a relationship, of course.

"What I mean is, I didn't tell you that the fellows were harmless and that they just like to play dominos for fun.

There isn't any gambling going on—at least not that I know of—so you can leave your broom in the closet."

Well, that did it. The pretty girl's smile went south, and the bristle returned to her backbone. "I thank you for that apology, Sheriff Wilson, however backhanded it turned out." She folded her napkin pretty as you please and set it on the table beside her coffee cup. "Now if you'll excuse me, I have work to do."

Rising, she beat a quick path to the door.

"What?" he called after her. "What did I say? Can't a man apologize?"

Lula came to the door, her hands white with flour. "Rafe, if I didn't know better, I'd think you meant to get off on the wrong foot with that girl."

"I did no such thing," he said. "Besides, I was just trying to tell her I was sorry."

Without comment, she turned and headed back to the kitchen, leaving Rafe to contemplate the unfairness of it all. Then he spotted the biscuit under the table.

There it sat, perfectly preserved atop a napkin that had fallen under the banker's chair. Neither milk nor humans had touched it, or at least it looked that way as he scooped it up and set it before him.

He was hungry as a bear and had the growl in his gut to

prove it. And there sat the butter and honey. Two minutes later the biscuit was in his hand and his boots were heading down Main Street.

"Miss Potter," he called as he trod lightly on her freshly mopped floor. "You in here?" A sound from the back of the building told him he wasn't alone. "Miss Potter?"

He set the biscuit on the first clean shelf he could find and headed off in the direction of the noise. This time he crept softly, not caring to let whoever was hiding there know he was coming.

To be safe, he palmed his revolver. As he felt the cold metal touch his palm, his heart kicked up a notch. The last time he used his gun, it had been for target practice. He hadn't missed then, and he wouldn't miss now.

Regulating his breath to cause the least amount of noise, Rafe hunkered down behind the counter and readied the weapon for firing. No common criminal would get away with trying to steal from Peony Potter.

Not with Rafe Wilson on duty.

Chapter 7

Pulse racing, Rafe slowly moved toward the back of the store. Again he heard movement—this time just beyond a large stack of newsprint.

"One last chance to come out before I have to carry you out."

"Sheriff, what are you doing?"

Rafe nearly jumped out of his skin. He whirled around to see Peony Potter standing behind him. "Get down and be quiet," he stated firmly.

To her credit, she complied without question.

A rustling sound preceded a loud crash, all taking place in the back of the store. Rafe touched his finger to Miss Potter's lips to indicate he needed silence in order to rid the shop of its intruder.

The next series of events happened in a blur. Rafe rushed the back room, gun ready. A movement caught his attention, and he aimed. Before he could shoot, someone or something knocked the weapon out of his hand. He fell, and a blur flew over him. His revolver skidded to a stop against the far wall, and Rafe scrambled after it.

By the time he retrieved his weapon and prepared to fire, he stood alone. Slowly he made his way through the debris into the main room. "Miss Potter?" he whispered.

No answer.

He clutched the weapon and strode toward the door. If the creep had harmed Miss Potter, well, Rafe would not be responsible for what he did when he caught up with him.

Two steps from the boardwalk, Peony Potter raced in and slammed into his chest. The collision sent him reeling backward while the dressmaker fell forward. Rafe rolled out of the way just in time to miss being landed on.

His gaze met hers, and to his surprise, she began to giggle. "What's so funny?"

Rather than respond, she pointed to a spot behind him. Rafe rolled over to see a fat orange cat with mismatched ears perched on a shelf.

"A cat?" The lop-eared feline looked about as happy as a

woodpecker in a petrified forest. Peony continued to giggle, and Rafe joined her. "I nearly shot a cat."

"Actually I think the cat won the battle." She pointed to his face.

Rafe swept the back of his hand over his cheek and came away with a smear of blood. Peony offered him a lacy handkerchief, which he reluctantly accepted. Replacing his revolver in his holster, Rafe leaned back against the counter and dabbed at his cheek.

"Miss Potter," he said as he exhaled, "this is by far the most exciting breakfast I think I've ever had."

"Breakfast?" She shook her head. "We missed breakfast, remember?"

Rafe searched the room for signs of Lula's napkin, finally spying a glimpse of the fabric beneath the overturned stack of newsprint. He reached to reclaim the treasure, only to find it hadn't survived the near-battle with the cat.

Inside the folded napkin, Lula's tasty biscuit had become a puddle of crumbs.

"Well, I tried," he said with a shrug.

Peony nodded. "I appreciate the effort, Sheriff. Remind me to call you if I need my breakfast smashed or my cat frightened to death."

He waited to see if she was making a joke, then laughed

when her expression showed she was. "I wish I'd known you had a cat."

Peony shrugged. "I didn't know I had one either."

Silence fell between them, giving Rafe time to study his companion. Indeed she was prettier than a newborn calf. A fellow could get used to looking at a woman like her.

Sure, they'd hit a rough patch early on in their getting-to-know-yous, but she looked as though she'd forgotten all about the little run-in with Pop and his ranger buddies.

Maybe it was time to let her know he'd felt something from the first time he laid eyes on her. He'd have to go slow, obviously, because a woman of Miss Potter's breeding probably wouldn't take kindly to a big oaf declaring his infatuation after such a short time.

No, he'd speak kindly of her first, greasing the path to her heart with a little flattery and a smile. He began with the smile. Obviously she liked what she saw, because it seemed she leaned a bit closer. He did his part and scooted in her direction. Between the leaning and the scooting, they soon found themselves side by side.

Oh, but she did smell good. A gentleman shouldn't wonder what it would be like to kiss a total stranger. But then, he and Miss Potter had been properly introduced by Millie, and she'd been approved of by Lula.

She had told him so in the kitchen just a short while ago. He'd laughed then. He wasn't laughing now.

Neither was she.

"Miss Potter, I want you to know that as sheriff of Cut Corners I've seen my share of—"

"I tell you, Stone, if you don't pay attention you're going to lose."

Pop.

Rafe groaned and inched a bit closer to the dressmaker. "As I was saying, Miss Potter, I've noticed that when you—"

"Honestly, gentlemen, a meeting of the town council's a serious matter. Why are you two worrying about the pickle barrel?"

Chaps this time. Miss Potter's face told Rafe she'd heard him, too.

Rafe sucked in a deep breath and let it out slowly, then debated stealing a kiss right then and there. He decided to show his gentlemanly side instead. "Miss Potter, what I'm trying to say is—"

"Now there you go trying to cheat, Eb Wilson. Didn't you think I'd notice?"

Swede.

No need to look at Miss Potter to know how cold the room had turned. He chanced a glance anyway. Any thoughts of stealing a kiss fled. Yep, better to make a quick exit than to sit here any longer and be thought a fool.

"I ought to be moseying on then," he said as he climbed to his feet and cast about for his hat. He found it on the floor beside the ladder and jammed it on his head.

Rafe had nearly made his exit when Miss Potter called to him. She remained seated on the floor, leaning against the counter, and he had to backtrack his steps to see her properly. To his amazement, the orange menace had jumped down from its perch on the shelf and made itself at home in her lap. She sat there scratching its good ear, a blank look on her face.

"Sheriff," she said as she met his stare, "thank you for breakfast."

Relief flooded him. "You're most welcome. I just wish I'd delivered it in one piece."

She nodded. "Yes, well, I appreciate the thought anyway."

Nodding, Rafe stood waiting for further praise or a word of any kind. Instead, the woman who'd set his heart to thumping remained quiet.

"Well then, I'll just be going."

Again she nodded. This time he got all the way outside before he turned to see her standing a distance behind him. "Sheriff," she said as she walked slowly toward him, "I'd appreciate it if you'd do me one favor."

By now she was close enough to smell her, and she smelled like lilacs. "What's that?" he asked.

"Seeing as how you take your job so seriously, I'd appreciate it if you'd do what you ought to and rid the streets of those four."

He didn't have to look over in the direction of where she pointed to know she referred to Pop and the boys. "Miss Potter, you're a fine lady, and I have thoroughly enjoyed most of the morning I've spent with you, but I believe you're out of line in asking me to remove the founding fathers of Cut Corners while they're holding a council meeting." He tipped his hat. "Now if you'll excuse me, I'll just go find some real law work to do. And to think I almost kissed you."

She huffed and puffed and stormed inside. "To think I almost let you."

Chapter 8

December 4, 1878

The Lord must have known Rafe wasn't meant to put down roots in Cut Corners, or He wouldn't have made the week in San Antonio such a productive one.

Rafe thought he probably should have signed the induction papers while he was there, but Captain Phelps urged him to take them home and think on it a spell first.

To his mind, there was nothing to think on. He was born to be a ranger; the Lord made him to follow in his father's footsteps. Why, then, did he feel as jumpy as a frog on a hot skillet about leaving the place he'd spent the past seven years?

True, Captain Phelps had given him the lecture about how hard it was to be a ranger and a family man. Well, he knew about that firsthand, but spending long periods of time with Pop away on duty hadn't killed him.

Could be his strange inability to get Peony Potter out of his mind. While he'd managed to steer clear of her for the better part of a month, his brain went goofy and his heart thudded whenever he thought of her. On those occasions when he found himself in the vicinity of her or her dress shop, he took pains to keep from having any actual conversations.

Trouble was, whenever he looked at her, he thought about kissing her. Whatever had transpired between them in the rubble of the old newspaper office had long since been forgotten by the dressmaker. That much was obvious on those rare occasions when he caught sight of her and she crossed the street to keep from having to say hello.

Rafe stepped off the train and waved to Ticks McGee over at the telegraph office. Making a passing glance in the direction of the dressmaker's shop, Rafe noted that in his absence the dressmaker had added a fluff of lace curtains in her front window and a neatly lettered sign reminding the ladies the time was at hand to order dresses for the Christmas social season.

What Christmas social season? Little did the silly Miss

Potter know, but the closest thing Cut Corners had to a holiday social gathering at all was the Christmas Eve pot roast special at Millie's Diner. Given the skill of the cook, or rather the lack of same, that postchurch gathering could hardly be described as a social event. The family party to celebrate his birthday generally didn't fare any better, as Millie tended to keep her cake recipes too high on the shelf to go by most years.

Bless her heart, dear Millie did try though, and thanks to her, he'd never spent a birthday feeling unloved or alone. Christmas Day was the one day of the year Pop and his buddies were always home.

As for Millie's pot roast, however, a single man ate what he could batch up in his own kitchen before he succumbed to the infamous Christmas Eve lunch, often seasoned up with sugar and other things your average cook wouldn't think of throwing in the skillet. But then Millie was not your average cook. The only reason tradition held was because being with others suffering the same fate seemed a slight bit better than suffering through another Christmas Eve alone in bachelor's quarters.

Rafe heard his father's laughter before he rounded the corner and caught sight of his pa and the others. Seated at their usual spot, the men looked to be plotting trouble—their usual state of affairs. Rafe slowed his pace and absentmindedly palmed the barrel of the revolver strapped to his hip.

The gun still saw less use than a mirror in a pigsty, but as sheriff, he wore it all the same. Actually he did shoot the thing occasionally in the line of duty. Just last year he'd had to fire off a round to scare a half dozen hogs that were feasting on the remains of the preacher's garden. Before that, he'd be hard-pressed to think of the last time he used a bullet on anything more dangerous than the tin cans he kept around for target practice.

A sorry state of affairs for a man who called himself a sheriff.

"Well, I don't see another way around it." His father again. "He simply ain't gonna be convinced lessen we take action."

"Who's not going to be convinced?" Rafe looked down into four of the guiltiest innocent faces he'd seen all week. "And what action are you planning to take?"

He turned first to the guiltiest of the lot, his father. "Pop, have you been reading my mail again?"

Eb Wilson had the decency to look offended, except that the expression didn't quite make it to his eyes. They twinkled with glee even as he frowned.

"I've been busy all morning and hardly had a chance to sit down." His nudge of the fellow sitting to his left was almost imperceptible.

Almost but not quite.

"Ja," Swede said. "Eb's been helping me set fence posts all morning. We've barely had a chance to sit down."

"Is that right?"

A chorus of agreement rose among the men. Rafe turned his attention to Stone and Chaps. Neither would look him in the eye. Finally he swung his gaze back to Pop, who suddenly found a great interest in studying the domino in his palm. The edge of a telegram peeked out of his pocket, evidence to Rafe's mind that Eb Wilson and his pals had been meddling again.

"You're a full-grown man, Son," his father said. "Why in the world would I want to waste my time poking my nose into your business?"

"Because you've been meddling in my business ever since I was out of knee pants, Pop. So have the rest of you." He paused to let the others express their halfhearted outrage. At least his father hadn't denied the accusation. "Look, I'm full-grown and able to make my own decisions on whatever—"

The rest of his statement caught in his throat as Peony Potter, dressed in something pink and pretty, appeared in the window of the dressmaker's shop. He struggled to capture his escaping thoughts and herd them back in the direction they were supposed to go. Unfortunately, gaining his voice and speaking anything other than nonsense was like trying to scratch his ear with his elbow. It just couldn't be done.

Peony looked over in his direction, and for a moment he thought she might wave. Instead, she looked past him to the four old rangers, then slammed the curtains shut.

"That girl's about as sociable as an ulcerated back tooth." Rafe didn't realize he'd spoken the comment aloud until the four meddling men hooted with laughter.

"She's as harmless as a bee in butter, Son." Pop rose to slap Rafe on the back. "All she needs is a little attention from the right man, and she'd be sweet as honey." He glanced down at his partners in crime, then winked at Rafe. "Maybe you ought to be the fellow who turns her attention to something besides criticizing decent folk for minding their own business on a public boardwalk."

Chuckling, Rafe pointed to his father. "You're the one with all the answers, Pop. Why don't you go smooth talk her?"

"I would, Son, but out of respect for the young, I thought I might give you a chance." He settled back into his chair and looked up at Rafe with a smug grin. "Lessen you don't think you're up to a challenge."

Any other challenge he would have taken in a split second. This one, however, he knew he'd never meet. Peony Potter had taken a dislike to him that time had not changed one lick. Better the subject moved on to something less ticklish.

"So, Pop, what's that in your pocket?"

Eb Wilson patted his chest. "This? Why, it looks like a telegram."

"Anything I ought to know about? Maybe something that beat me here from San Antonio?" He gave his best shot at looking like a lawman deep in the midst of a serious investigation. "I know you and your buddies at the ranger command post are still thick as thieves. You got something you want to 'fess up to?"

The older man seemed to consider his question for a moment. His pals watched him without expression. Rafe had to give it to the four of them. These old rangers might be slowed by age, but not a one of them showed any signs of weakness when questioned.

"Something to 'fess up to? I don't reckon so." His father's grin widened. "Besides, we all know Ticks McGee can't keep a secret. If it was anything important, you'd have heard about it before you stepped out of the depot."

This much was true. The telegraph operator could best any woman in town in a gossiping contest.

"You all in agreement with Pop? Nothing new I need to hear about?" The other three nodded, although Rafe noted that none of them could quite look him in the eyes. "Then I guess you aren't interested in what I told your old buddy Captain Phelps when he asked me if I could report for duty with the rangers the first Monday in January."

With that, he tipped his hat and walked away.

Chapter 9

Peony stepped back from the curtains and watched the sheriff move with purposeful strides toward the building that housed the jail. "That man makes me so mad."

Peony spoke to the orange lop-eared cat that had taken up residence in her shop during the former owner's absence, the same cat that had almost lost its life to the sheriff's bullet. Naming the feline Tabby, Peony appreciated the fuzzy guest's listening ear. Who else could she complain to about a man who was obviously the paragon of virtue and respect in Cut Corners?

She'd mentioned to Mrs. Chamberlain, the owner of the boardinghouse, that she'd been irritated at the lack of concern the lawman showed in ridding the streets of the riffraff only to find out the woman had practically raised him and thought he hung the moon. A discussion with Millie over breakfast regarding the men who insisted on gambling within earshot of her establishment resulted in bitter coffee and cold flapjacks. Of course, in dear Millie's case, that could have been the norm and not any sort of statement regarding her opinion.

Sighing, Peony lifted a stack of neatly folded fabric onto the shelf nearest the door, then stood back and admired her handiwork. In no time, she'd managed to get the former newspaper office clean and orderly and had even pried the boards off the window in the back to allow the morning sun to shine in.

That last feat had been accomplished with ease. It was amazing what a woman could do when she was angry. Why, if she lived to be a hundred and ten, she never would understand men.

Especially that man.

Shuddering at the reminder of the cranky lawman, she forced her mind to the task at hand. Soon a pretty yellow calico dress wore bright green buttons and a thick set of seams down the side. The newly expectant farm wife who ordered the garment would have plenty of room to let it out once her belly began to swell.

Peony allowed the dress to slip from her fingers. For a moment, she allowed herself the luxury of imagining what it might be like to be some man's wife, some child's mother. As quickly as the image appeared, she chased it away with thoughts of the next project on her list: unpacking the newest parcel of fabrics from Dallas.

She pushed the ancient rolling ladder—a welcome leftover from the previous owner—closer, then climbed to reach the topmost shelf. Peony settled a stack of multicolored calicos atop the shelf and climbed down to retrieve a basket of thread.

Unfortunately Tabby had taken up residence inside, and she complained bitterly when Peony ousted her onto the floor. The cat gave her an irritated look, then turned tail and headed for the crate that held Peony's unpacked sewing machine.

A cackle of male laughter followed by four distinct voices all speaking at once assailed her through the front windows. Those awful gamblers again. This time, due to threatening skies, they seemed to be headed for Millie's Diner.

"Believe me, we all have our irritations, Tabby," Peony said as she hefted the basket onto her shoulder and stepped onto the ladder. "At least you can find another place where you won't be bothered. I don't have that luxury."

Not with the sheriff refusing to do his job.

His job. Peony shook her head. Well, of course the man wasn't doing his job. The ringleader of the gamblers was his father. She'd found that out over breakfast one morning in the diner.

And the other three, well, to hear Lula tell it, they were practically family, as well. Of course the man was loyal to those he cared for, an admirable trait under most circumstances. Oh, how she disliked admitting he had good traits.

"Excuse me, ma'am, but might I have a word with you?"

Peony looked up to see Eb Wilson standing on the porch looking in. He seemed out of place, a rough man among laces and calico, and his demeanor showed he felt that way, too.

Mama might have done a lot of things wrong, but one thing she did right was to teach Peony respect for her elders. "Please, do come in," she said, rising to meet him halfway. "Would you like some tea? I was just about to make myself some."

The older man clutched his hat in his hands and studied the boardwalk. "No, ma'am, and if you don't mind, I believe I'll just stand out here. Fancy stuff makes me nervous."

Suppressing a smile, she took a few steps forward. "How can I help you, Mr. Wilson?"

"Well now, it's me who's aiming to help you, actually."

He lifted his gaze to meet hers. "It's about my boy, Rafe. I believe you two are acquainted."

Irritation rose. "Yes, we've had several conversations," she said.

"And I feel bad about that, ma'am. I believe my friends and I are the source of those conversations, and I'd like to apologize right now for that."

"You would?"

He nodded. "You see, it's come to my attention that the friction between you and my boy might be the cause of him not telling you his true feelings."

Ticks McGee appeared in the doorway of the mercantile across the way. Peony offered the man a polite wave, then turned her attention back to Mr. Wilson.

"What do you mean 'his true feelings'?"

"Miss Potter, I'm a single man myself, have been for nigh on twenty-seven years now, but when my Carolina was alive, rest her soul, well. . ." He paused to clear his throat. "Let's just say I remember what it felt like to be in love, and I feel terrible that I might be keeping you two apart."

"I assure you, Mr. Wilson, you are not keeping us apart."

Eb Wilson let out a yell that caused the horses tied in front of the bank to skitter and complain. He took a step inside to clasp Peony's hand and shake it with vigor. "Now that's the best thing I've heard all day."

"It is?"

"Yes, indeed. Thank you for clearing that up, Miss Potter." He set his hat back firmly on his head. "I believe I'll go let Rafe know he doesn't have to hide his affections any longer." With a wink, he added, "You have a lovely afternoon, you hear?"

Peony stood in the door and watched the elder Mr. Wilson cross Main Street with a spring in his step. Tipping his hat to Ticks McGee, he headed in the direction of the sheriff's office.

A plaintive meow reminded Peony that she wasn't alone in the dress shop. She turned to see Tabby sunning herself beneath the lace curtains and knelt to scratch the soft fur behind the cat's right ear. The cat stretched and nestled against her hand.

"Now that was an interesting conversation."

❧

Rafe leaned back in his chair, resting the heels of his boots on his desk. He need not worry about disturbing the contents of its surface with his big feet. There hadn't been anything of value sitting on the scarred wooden surface since he took the job back in '71.

Hearing from the rangers had been the only bright spot in his week—his year, actually—and just thinking about getting out from behind this desk to ride with them gave him a smile. Only his pop's strange reluctance to discuss the matter kept him from jumping for joy.

Why Eb Wilson couldn't be proud that his only son wanted to join the family business was beyond him. It was a plain fact that Pop and his buddies only left the rangers because the government folks disbanded the units and sent their men off to fight in the War between the States. Pop never talked about why the three of them chose to settle in Cut Corners and take up the ordinary life of gentlemen farmers and such after the war ended. When pressed to comment, Eb's response was always the same: "I made a promise."

What sort of promise or to whom remained a mystery to this day, one Rafe had chosen not to try and solve. For whatever reason, his father gave up a life of adventure and purpose to loll about a small town with little to do but play dominoes with his buddies and rehash the old days. The funny thing was, this man who once captained a unit of fearless lawmen seemed perfectly content sitting in front of the old newspaper office until it got too dark to see the checkerboard.

Only a heavy rain or Sunday services broke up the rhythm of the day for the old codgers. Worse, they seemed to like it that way.

"Well, that's not for me," Rafe muttered as he leaned back a notch farther and settled his hat over his eyes to begin his morning nap. "This man's going places."

"Well, not today, you ain't."

Chapter 10

Rafe jerked to attention and caught his hat before it hit the floor. His pop stood in the doorway. He half expected at least one of Pop's cronies to be standing with him. The fact that he showed up alone could only mean one thing.

Here it comes. The lecture about being content. So much for the nap.

With a heavy sigh, he placed both feet firmly on the floor. Resisting the urge to speak, he merely stared. As much as he loved his father, he had no desire to have his good mood ruined by the contentment lecture. Come Christmas Day, he'd be twenty-seven years old. If that wasn't too old to be told what to do, then he'd eat his hat.

Besides, he was content, wasn't he? There were only a few things in his life he really wanted to change. If a man was looking to hang his hat somewhere besides Cut Corners and to get his pay from someone other than the mayor of this fair city, where was the fault in that?

"Ain't you going to ask what's wrong, Son?"

"I reckon you're going to tell me whether I ask or not." Once again, Rafe sighed. At times like this, he wished he hadn't heard the Lord's command on honoring your father. He loved Eb Wilson more than anything on this earth, but the man could sorely try his patience. "Why don't you come on over here and sit a spell and tell me what's on your mind?"

"Maybe I will."

Pop sauntered over and stood a minute before settling himself into the chair on the other side of the desk. He made a fuss of rubbing the stubble on his jawbone before turning his gaze on Rafe. "You really aim to do it this time, don't ya?"

"Do what, Pop? Sign up for the rangers?" When his father nodded, Rafe continued. "I wish you'd just come right out and tell me what's so bad about your son following in your footsteps."

"I'll admit I'm right pleased that you would consider the rangers, but it's just that. . ." His father lapsed into silence, a pained look on his face.

Understanding dawned, and along with it, anger. Rafe rose and steadied himself with a firm grip on the corner of the desk.

"Say it, Pop," he managed through clenched jaw. "You don't think I can make a ranger of myself."

Eb Wilson fairly flew out of his chair. "That's the most ridiculous thing I heard come out of anyone's mouth. I'm proud as I can be of you."

Rafe frowned. His father looked like he was about to bust his buttons. "You sure about that?"

"Son, if anybody was cut out to be a ranger, it was you. Why, from the time you were knee-high to a grasshopper, you could ride and shoot with the best of 'em."

"That's because I learned from the best, Pop." He shrugged. "So, you admit I'm qualified. What's your beef with me signing up?"

His father looked like he planned to jaw on that question awhile, so it surprised Rafe that he spoke right up. "Well now, there's two things wrong with the plan. First off, you're needed right here in Cut Corners." Before Rafe could protest, Pop held up his hand to silence him. "You asked; now hear me out. This town needs a lawman who will keep the criminal element out. It can't be helped that the place is as quiet as a Monday morning church house. You ought not complain because you're doing such a good job. Come January if you're not here, what do you think will happen? You think anyone's going to protect Lula and Millie and Miss Potter and the others like you do? I say not."

"I never thought of it that way, Pop."

A satisfied look crossed the older man's face. "Well, you chew on that thought awhile. "You'll be missed. In fact, the boys and I are so sure that you're needed that we drew up a little something we'd like you to sign." He pulled the folded sheet of paper—the one Rafe had thought was a telegram—out of his pocket and thrust it in Rafe's direction. "It's a little contract Chaps drew up. We'd all be obliged if you'd sign it."

"Now hold on a minute. I don't know about this. Since when does the sheriff of Cut Corners operate under a contract?"

Pop shrugged. "Since this morning." He stood. "Look here, boy, I know you're aiming to feel your oats, but I got a notion that what you want isn't out there on the trail. No, I think the thing to set your heart to thumping ain't a thing or even a job. I think it's a woman."

"What are you talking about? Captain Phelps thinks—"

"Son, I don't care what Captain Phelps thinks. Until you handle things with Miss Potter, you're not going to be worth the saddle you ride in. You'll be forever trying to prove something." Regret washed over his wrinkled features. "I love you, boy, but you need to find out your heart's right here before you go running all over Texas looking for it and missing out on what's right here."

"Pop, you're talking foolish now."

"Am I? That woman's crazy about you, and I can't help but see that you feel the same way. There, I've said it." With that, he stormed outside and left Rafe with his mouth hanging open.

"Hold on a minute, Pop." Rafe jumped to his feet and followed his father out the door. "You really believe all that, or is this just one more case of meddling?"

Eb Wilson stopped and whirled around, nearly causing Lionel Sager's sister, Vivian, to plow right into him. Sidestepping the girl, Pop headed back in Rafe's direction, only stopping when he was practically under Rafe's nose.

The two men stood eye-to-eye. Neither blinked.

"Rafael Wilson, you are a good man, born of good stock, and well loved by your mama, who's now in heaven, rest her soul. I've loved you and cared for you, and I've been blessed to have the help of Lula and Millie to raise you. In all those years, have I ever meddled in your affairs?"

"Yes. Frequently."

"Fair enough. In this case, however, I'm going to step back and give you just enough rope to hang yourself. That contract on your desk is the key to your happiness, boy. You're a better lawman than any ranger who ever rode, me included, but that don't mean you have to leave the ones who loved you and raised you. Your talents are needed right here. Why, you never know when there's going to be some big threat to your loved ones. Where will you be when that happens—here or somewhere else?"

He paused to catch a long breath. Rafe dared not speak. He didn't like the choice of words floating around in his brain. Half were disrespectful, the rest downright frightening in that if he said them he'd be agreeing with Pop.

"Now, the other thing. I aim to state that youth is wasted on the young. Why, if I had a pretty filly like Miss Potter watching my every move, I sure wouldn't be spending my spare time over at Erik Olson's carpenter shop hammering nails and sawing table legs."

"Pop, you don't know what you're talking about. That woman hates me. She's made that fact plain enough."

Pop chuckled. "I repeat. Youth is wasted on the young. Why do you think she pays so much attention to you if she isn't sweet on you?" He shook his head. "Why, your mama, rest her soul, gave me such grief when I first started showing up on her doorstep that any sane man would have turned tail and run."

"Is that right?"

"That's right. Now the question is, what do you think about that girl? You sweet on her? I bet you can't look into her eyes without your heart going pitty-pat."

"Yes I can." Lately, anyway. But then, he'd made it a practice to avoid her.

"Well, you answered that awful fast. What is it Shakespeare says—'Methinks thou dost protest too much'?" He clapped a hand on Rafe's shoulder. "Look, I don't aim to tell anyone about how you think Miss Potter's prettier than a new calf on a spring morning. I do think maybe you ought to let her know that."

"But I don't think that," he said as he watched Pop's back disappear down the boardwalk. "I really don't think that."

But did he believe what he said? There was only one way to find out. He'd take Pop up on his challenge. He'd go right down there to the dressmaker's shop and look her in the eyes and prove to himself and Pop that Peony Potter was the last woman in the world for him.

First he ought to head home and change shirts.

"Well?" Chaps said. "What happened? Did you talk to him?"

Eb smiled and leaned across the checkerboard. The other three followed suit.

"I spoke my piece." He paused for effect. "To both of 'em."

Stone's eyes narrowed. "How'd they take it?"

"About like I expected." Eb turned to Chaps. "Everything set?"

Chaps nodded. "Ticks ought to be getting the telegram any minute."

"Why'd you send Ticks a telegram?" Stone asked.

"I didn't." Chaps grinned. "I sent myself one. You know how Ticks is. The news of that secret gold shipment will be all over town before sundown. The rest of you done what you were supposed to?"

The three men nodded. "I predict there will be a veritable crime spree in Cut Corners in short order."

"Hello, Miss Potter." Eb smiled at the dressmaker as she passed them on the boardwalk and stepped inside her shop. "Lovely afternoon we're having, isn't it?"

Peony Potter paused to glanced over her shoulder. Without saying a word, she gave him a look that left no doubt she'd heard everything they said. Eb waited for the woman to say something.

To his surprise, she merely smiled and disappeared inside the shop.

He reached over to slap Chaps on the back. "I like that girl," he said. "She's going to be good for Rafe."

Chapter 11

"Y ou didn't hear it from me, Miss Potter, but there's a secret shipment of gold headed through Cut Corners."

Peony looked up from her needlework to offer Ticks McGee a smile. He had wasted no time delivering the telegram to the British fellow, but it seemed as though he might spend the rest of the afternoon sitting in Peony's shop. Unlike the elder Mr. Wilson, this man had no reservations about sipping tea in such a feminine setting.

Perhaps she shouldn't have offered him that second cup. She couldn't help herself, as the man was a wealth of information. Today his topic was the safety of Cut Corners and Rafe Wilson's ability to defend the entire town from marauders should the need arise.

"Why I've seen that man fend off a dozen wild boar with a single-shot rifle." He fiddled with the chain of his pocket watch, then smiled. "Very impressive if I do say so myself."

"Now Ticks, you know there were only a half dozen of them, and they were hogs, not wild boar." Rafe tipped his hat and nodded toward Peony. "Afternoon, Miss Potter."

"Mr. Wilson."

Ticks scrambled to his feet, very nearly upsetting the contents of his teacup.

"Might I have a word with the lady, Ticks?"

The telegraph officer nodded and continued to sip his tea.

"Alone," Rafe added.

With that, Ticks set his cup on the table and beat a path to the door. As soon as they were alone, Rafe's expression softened.

"Miss Potter, I thought I ought to tell you that I've come to a decision about my future. You see, I—"

"Rafe, is that you?"

He turned to wave at a blond-haired gentleman. As he neared the door, Peony recognized Erik Olson.

"Am I interrupting something?" he asked.

The sheriff shook his head, and a look of relief flooded his face. "Naw, I was just passing the time of day with Miss

Potter. Miss Potter, do you know my friend Erik? He's the carpenter here in town."

She nodded. "Yes, in fact, he's working on some plans for the shop, aren't you, Mr. Olson?"

"Ja," the blond giant said. "Well, I have come to speak to Rafe, but I can do that another time."

"No, really, I was just leaving," Sheriff Wilson said. "Best regards, Miss Potter."

Before she could respond, he and the carpenter were gone. "Thanks," she heard him say as she skittered to the window to watch them walk away.

"For what?" the carpenter responded.

The sheriff's reply was drowned out by the cackle of the men sitting at the domino table mere feet from her window. Closing the lace curtains with a huff, she headed to the back of the shop to find something, anything, to do.

❦

"My friend, you are the best employee I have ever had. I do not even mind that you are only here to hide from Miss Potter."

"That's not true, Erik. I like working with my hands. It feels good to accomplish something." Rafe looked up from the chair he'd just nailed back together and smiled. "Well, I admit that Miss Potter hasn't thought to look for me here, but I am the only employee you've ever had, and I work for free." He righted the chair, then sat in it. "And I'm not hiding from Miss Potter. I just don't happen to want her to find me anytime soon."

"Is she still complaining about the rangers?" Erik chuckled. "It seems as though someone should have explained the situation to her by now. Those four men are the reason Cut Corners exists. If they want to set up a checkerboard and play a few games, they ought to be left alone to do it."

"You and I think so, but the new dressmaker disagrees. And because she disagrees, I haven't had a decent nap in more than two weeks."

"Well now," Erik said as he shook the wood shavings out of his hair, "I thought you were here because you wanted something constructive to do with your spare time. I did not realize it was insomnia that drove you across the street."

"Just don't get used to the extra help. I'll be gone before you know it."

Erik stopped his sanding work on Parson Clune's new pulpit and straightened his back. "You are really going to join up with the rangers?"

Nodding, Rafe slapped his knees and rose. "What? You look like you swallowed a bug, Erik. You know I'm expected at headquarters after the first of the year. Did you think I'd change my mind?"

"Actually, I did." His friend began to chuckle. A moment later he rose to slap Rafe on the back. "Rafe Wilson, a Texas Ranger. Now that is something to celebrate."

Rafe held up his hand. "It's a little early to celebrate. I haven't officially accepted yet."

"Accepted what?" Jeff strolled into the workshop. "Did I miss a good story?"

"Rafe is joining up with the rangers," Erik said. "Evidently he is not happy repairing chairs and building bookcases for a living."

"I'm a lawman," Rafe said, "and I need to go where a lawman is needed."

Jeff shook his head. "Your pop's not going to like this."

"My pop's going to be so proud of me that he can't stand it." Rafe pushed the chair out of his way and settled his hat back on his head. "Besides, we talked about it when I came back from my visit with Captain Phelps. He was fine with it then, and he will be fine with it now."

"If that's so, why haven't you told him when you're leaving yet?" Jeff asked.

"I'll tell him soon enough." Rafe strode past his cousin to regard his friend. "I appreciate being put to work here, Erik. Good, honest labor makes a man feel useful."

And I haven't felt useful in a very long time.

"Where are you headed?" Jeff called as he trotted to catch up.

"I thought I might have a word with Pop," Rafe said as his cousin fell into step beside him.

Jeff nodded. "Want some company?"

He pondered the question for a moment. "I probably ought to do this by myself. I don't know what's gotten into Pop, but every time I try to mention talking to Captain Phelps or joining up with the rangers, he changes the subject. It's downright perplexing."

"I've noticed he is a might tight-lipped on the subject," Jeff said. "Maybe he's missing the good old days when he and the others rode with the rangers. Have you ever wondered what they'd be doing now if the rangers hadn't been disbanded back in the sixties?"

"Mr. Wilson."

Rafe and Jeff turned in unison to see the dressmaker standing on the boardwalk a few feet away. Rafe suppressed a groan. For the better part of two weeks, he'd managed to avoid the tiny terror; now there she stood. Too late to turn tail and run, not that retreat ever set well with him.

So far, however, he'd managed to either hide or head for the hills every time she came around the office complaining.

Someone must have told her by now that the sheriff and the chief offender at the checkers table were father and son. Did she honestly expect him to run Pop and his buddies out of town on a rail?

"Sheriff Wilson."

"That's what I was afraid of," Rafe muttered. Out of the corner of his eye, he saw Jeff slink away toward the black-smith shop and wished he could join him. "How can I help you, Miss Potter?"

"Rafe! Rafe Wilson, come on over here right now. There's been a robbery!" Millie trotted toward him, both hands in the air. "Come quick, Rafe; someone's done stole my pies."

"Rafe Wilson, is that you?"

Rafe whirled around to see Parson Clune standing on the boardwalk behind him. The preacher looked more flustered than Millie, a rare state of affairs for the sedate man. "Rafe, someone's stolen my tomato plants right out of the ground. Why, I just put those plants in the ground two days ago. Come with me, and I'll show you the scene of the crime."

"Begging your pardon, Parson Clune," Millie said, "but the scene of the crime's over at my place. Three pies gone right off the counter."

"Sheriff, I really must have a word with you," Miss Potter said.

"Well, wait your turn," Millie scolded. "I've got a crime scene in my diner."

Parson Clune pointed over his shoulder to the church. "Forgive me, Millie, but I've got a crime scene in my garden, too."

"Rafe, is that you? Would you mind stepping over here a minute?"

He swung his attention to the mercantile where Lionel Sager stood on the boardwalk waving. "Yes, it's me," he said. "I'm a little busy right now, though."

"Well, I'm in need of the law, and you're the only law in Cut Corners."

Rafe pushed his hat back a notch on his head and focused on the mercantile owner. "What do you need the law for, Lionel?"

"Pickles. Someone took 'em all. Every last one of them."

"Excuse me, Sheriff," the dressmaker said.

Suppressing a frown, he let out a long breath. "Not now, Miss Potter. Your complaints can wait. We have real crimes here."

"Actually, that's exactly what I was going to tell you." She peered up at him from beneath the brim of a ruffled bonnet just a shade darker than her eyes, eyes that looked like they were about to fill with tears. "Perhaps you and I might continue this conversation at a later date. Much later. In fact, I think I'd rather not have a conversation with you at all, thank you very much." With that, she swung her skirts toward the dressmaker's shop and disappeared inside.

"Sheriff!"

Chapter 12

December 17, 1878

It took Rafe the better part of two weeks to solve the mystery of the crime wave in Cut Corners. At first he only had his suspicions, but when each of the crime victims awoke on Sunday morning to a bag of coins in the amount of their loss, he knew it had to be Pop and the boys. While the trouble they went to flattered him, he was tempted to throw them all in the jailhouse for a night to keep them from doing it again.

Instead, he settled for a formal apology from each one, in writing, and given to the crime victims in the middle of Main Street. The only citizen of Cut Corners missing that day was Peony Potter. By the time he got around to noticing, the event was over and the crowd had dispersed.

He ought to go make peace with her. If he did, he might end up losing out on the biggest adventure of his life. No, better to remain at odds with Peony Potter than to risk turning down Captain Phelps and the rangers in favor of spending more time with the pretty dressmaker.

"Sheriff, you got a plan for what's gonna happen when the stage rolls through on Christmas Eve?"

Rafe looked up from his musings to see Ticks McGee standing in his office. "If I got a plan, do you think I'm going to share it with you?"

Actually he only had the beginning of a plan, but he'd never admit that to Ticks. The gold shipment described in the telegram he'd received last Friday was so large, it would need four men to protect it. With Cut Corners set squarely on the trail to the gold's final destination, Rafe would be entrusted with seeing it safely through town.

He folded the telegram and slid it into his shirt pocket. As much as he hated it, it sure felt good to be doing some real sheriffing.

Of course, he'd be living the life of a real lawman soon enough. In the meantime, he had plans to make. The stage would be rolling through a week from today. Other than deputizing the four former rangers, his cousin Jeff, and Erik Olson, he hadn't had a chance to make good on any of the other details of the plan to protect the stage.

Rafe sighed as he unrolled the maps Pop had loaned him. This was going to be a big job, but he was up for the challenge.

"Excuse me, Sheriff Wilson." Peony Potter stood in the doorway. "May I come in?"

He motioned for her to come in, then returned his attention to his maps. When she settled in the chair opposite him, he realized he was in for a longer conversation than he'd hoped.

Ignoring her had never worked in the past, so he decided to get the confrontation out of the way right off. "Yes, I know, Pop and his buddies have been up to no good. File a written report and be on your way, please."

He was totally unprepared for her giggle. "You have no idea, Sheriff."

Leaning back in his chair, he regarded her from beneath the brim of his hat. "What are you talking about, Miss Potter?"

When she told him, he fairly fell off the chair. "So this is all a fake?"

She nodded. "It seems as though your father and his

friends are trying to show you that you belong in Cut Corners by creating some excitement that will culminate with a stage holdup."

"How do you know this for sure?"

"Remind me, Sheriff. Where do these men sit every day for hours on end?"

Rafe smiled. "Miss Potter, I would like to apologize for my father and his friends. It seems as though they have been up to no good, and I've allowed your customers to be exposed to it."

"You know, I believe I will accept your apology. Now what are we going to do about this?"

Ticks McGee ambled in with a telegram in his hand. "Sorry, folks, I was just passing through, and I had this telegram for Miss Potter and, well, I thought. . ."

Rafe rose and strolled to the other side of the desk, casually resting on the corner as he regarded the telegraph operator. "You thought you were going to catch me with Miss Potter?"

"Yes, actually," he said with a gulp.

Rafe looked down at Peony and winked. "And what did you think you would catch us doing?"

"N–n–nothing at all, Sheriff," he said as he backed out of the office and headed down the street.

"Miss Potter, I have a plan."

She rose. "Do you?"

He nodded. With your help, we are going to expose these old coots for the meddling men they are."

"I like that," she said.

"There's just one thing," he added.

"What's that?"

Rafe smiled. "I'm going to have to kiss you first."

"I thought you might say that."

"Any complaints if I do?"

"If I do, I'll put them in writing like you asked," she said as she leaned up on her tiptoes.

"Fair enough," he whispered just before their lips made contact and he lost his heart to Peony Potter.

Chapter 13

"Here it comes," Eb shouted. "There's the stage—right on time."

Rafe nodded and pointed to the west. "Jeff, you and Erik go that way. Pop, you and the fellows fall in behind the stage and escort it through town and on into the next county. I'll ride ahead and scout for trouble."

As the men rode off on their respective assignments, Rafe smiled. *Pop always has a plan. Let's see how he likes my plan.*

Just over the rise, Rafe spotted a pair of would-be robbers poised to hold up the stage. He'd pegged them as former ranger friends of Pop's, owing to his long memory and the recognizable faces of the pair.

A quick conversation with them along with an explanation and the pair were more than happy to deviate from the plan. Rafe waved as he passed the men, who now hid behind a stand of trees. As the stage rolled past, the two fellows gave chase.

The real fun began when Pop and the boys rode up behind the group and dismounted beside the stage. Hidden in the underbrush, Rafe watched the scene unfold. Pop jumped to the ground first and strolled toward the two fake robbers with the other three in hot pursuit. Just about the time the meddling men had gathered around the stage, they found themselves held at gunpoint.

"What are you doing, fellas?" Pop inquired as he was handed into the empty stage. "This isn't how the plan was supposed to work."

"Ja," Swede said. "You're not supposed to be taking us prisoner."

"Shut up and get inside," the taller of the pair shouted as he emptied the rangers' weapons of their bullets and tossed them into the bushes.

As the last of the men fell into the stage, the pair bolted the door and turned the stage north. "Where are you taking us?" Pop called.

On cue, Rafe rode up alongside the stage. "Hey, Pop," he called.

Eb Wilson stuck his head out of the stage and frowned. "What're you doing out there, boy? You turn crook on me?"

Rafe grinned. "Well, actually—"

A round of gunfire interrupted his words. The driver halted the stage as a pair of masked gunmen rode toward them.

"Very funny, Rafe," Chaps said. "But I think turning our own two against us was enough. You didn't have to add more actors to the game."

Rafe froze. "I don't know what you're talking about. I didn't have anything to do with those two."

A bullet zinged past, snaking a hole in Rafe's best hat before it lodged in the side of the stage. With the four former rangers disarmed and the two false robbers carrying guns that held no bullets, Rafe was the sole possessor of a working weapon.

The first bandit rode up at lightning speed, leveling his weapon as he passed. Rafe had no trouble knocking him out of his saddle with the first bullet. When the second criminal appeared, he too was felled by Rafe's revolver.

Releasing the four rangers from the confines of the stage, Rafe hung back and let Pop take a look at the two bad guys. "Yep, they won't be robbing any stages anytime soon," Pop said as he looked up at Rafe with admiration in his eyes. "That's some nice shooting. You brought 'em down but didn't kill 'em. Like as not, they'll wish you did after they stand trial." Pop reached up to shake Rafe's hand. "Son, you've proved to me you're more than fit to ride with the rangers."

"Pop, I appreciate that, but I was wondering something."

"What's that?"

He smiled. "I was wondering if one of you meddling men had a copy of that contract you gave me awhile back."

"Why's that?" Pop asked.

Rafe shrugged. "Oh, I don't know. I kind of thought I might stay right here in Cut Corners and see what sort of trouble I can get into."

Up ahead a buggy came over the rise. Rafe recognized it instantly as Lula Chamberlain's rig. Riding beside Lula was Peony Potter.

"And here comes that trouble now," Rafe said as he urged his horse into a gallop and met his future bride halfway.

At least he hoped she would be his future bride. First he had to ask her.

Epilogue

Christmas Day, 1878

R afe, there are things about my past you don't know."
Peony leaned against the tree just past the privy and
stared up at the light flakes of snow as they dusted the
sheriff's blue-black hair. "Things that might surprise you."

Rafe wiped a snowflake off Peony's nose and smiled. "I
can't imagine a thing that would make me love you any less."

He'd asked her to marry him just yesterday, presenting
the idea of the two of them living in Cut Corners and raising a family only a few minutes after he signed the contract
agreeing to be sheriff for another year. Peony had said yes
after joking that he was only spending the day with her to

avoid the bachelors' pot roast at Millie's Diner.

She'd been elated yesterday, but now she worried he might change his mind once he heard the full truth about her past.

Peony sighed. "I'm not really from Dallas like I led you to believe. I was raised in New Orleans, and my mama, well. . ." She paused to regard the man who'd stolen her heart. "If, after you hear this, you want to call off the wedding, I'll understand."

Stealing a quick kiss, Rafe shook his head. "I won't, but go ahead and tell me anyway."

So she did, starting with her papa's leaving them, her mama's occupation, and finally telling him about the dead man on the train headed for San Francisco. When she'd told the entire tale, she sat back and waited for Rafe to break the engagement.

Instead, he sat in silence for a moment. Finally he turned to face her. "Sounds like we both come from interesting families," he said as the sound of Pop and the boys echoed around them. "Now how about you and I go inside and have some birthday cake?"

"Millie's cake?"

He nodded.

"Can't we just stay out here a little longer?"

He stole one kiss, then two more. He would have stolen another except that he heard Millie calling his name. "Be right there, Millie," he said. "Just one more kiss."

"Happy Birthday, Rafe Wilson," Peony whispered. "And Merry Christmas. Looks like you are the marrying kind after all."

CHRISTMAS EVE BACHELORS' POT ROAST

2 tablespoons olive oil
1 clove garlic, minced
½ onion, chopped fine
Beef or pork roast, any size
Carrots, peeled and cut in 2" lengths
Onions, cut in eighths
Potatoes, quartered
2 cans golden mushroom soup

Place Dutch oven on burner set at medium-high. Heat olive oil and add garlic and onions. Sauté. Brown roast, then cover with vegetables and reduce heat. Prepare 2 cans mushroom soup per package directions, then pour evenly over roast and vegetables. Cover and let simmer 1–2 hours, depending on size of roast. Serve with rolls or corn bread.

KATHLEEN Y'BARBO

Kathleen Y'Barbo is an award-winning novelist and sixth-generation Texan. After completing a degree in marketing at Texas A&M University, she focused on raising four children and turned to writing. She is a member of American Christian Romance Writers, Romance Writers of America, and Writers Information Network. She also lectures on the craft of writing at the elementary and secondary levels, and conducts distance-learning classes on the university level.

Here Cooks the Bride

by Cathy Marie Hake

Chapter 1

September, 1879

"Excuse me, sir."

Jeff halted mid-motion, his shovel full of coal. Black dust swirled around his thick boots as he glanced at the young lady. Oh, and she was definitely a *lady*. Judging from her so-very-proper Boston accent, the Daddy-has-money traveling suit with all the fuss and bother, and her wide hazel eyes, this gal wasn't just out of place; she was lost.

"Might I impose for a moment to inquire as to the location of your local diner?"

He dumped the coal into his wheelbarrow and stood to

his full height. "Diner's closed. Best hop back aboard the train and try Meadsville."

The feather in her stylish hat swayed back and forth as she gave her head a small shake. "I fear I did not make myself known. I'm Lacey Mather, and I've come to help my great-aunt Millie at the diner."

"Millie's your great-aunt?" Jeff couldn't hide the surprise in his voice. On her better days, Millie looked as if she'd been caught in a whirlwind. Most of the time, she looked like she sorted bobcats for a living. No man in his right mind would imagine Millie as kin to this dainty blond beauty.

"Yes." Miss Mather folded her white-gloved hands at her waist and gave him a charming smile. "I'm eager to reacquaint myself with her. Could you please direct me to her place?"

"Sure. Go on through the station here, and you'll see Main Street turning off to the west from Ranger Road. Millie's is the first place on the right side of Main."

Miss Proper-and-Pretty leaned forward ever so slightly. "Would west be to my right or left?"

Jeff tamped down a groan. Helpless. The woman wasn't just lost, she was utterly helpless. What kind of assistance did she think she could give Millie, clear out here in the wilds of Texas? He heaved a sigh. "Give me a minute. I can show you the way—long as you don't mind coal dust."

Laughter tinkled out of her—from behind her gloved hand, of course. "Sir, after riding a train for the past three days, I assure you, I could shake out my skirts and fill your wheelbarrow!"

The woman had a point. He nodded, then directed, "There's a bench over yonder. I'll just be a minute."

Chestnut brown skirts whispered as she turned to walk away. The whisper might as well have been a shout, because the narrow-cut front of that fancy dress hadn't prepared him for this view. Row upon row of ruffles draped over a sassy bustle and spilled to the ground. Dainty, swaying steps led her away from the bench and toward a trunk, valise, and hatbox.

She really does plan to stay.

The realization made Jeff groan aloud. Bad enough that Millie couldn't cook a lick. Put both women in the kitchen, and most of Cut Corners would probably die of food poisoning. Resigned to continue to prepare his own meals, Jeff dumped more coal into his wheelbarrow and muttered, "Lord, I know I'm not supposed to question Your wisdom, but seems to me a homely old spinster who knew her way around a stove would be a much better choice for us here in Cut Corners."

The train whistle blew, adding an exclamation mark to his opinion.

"You've been too kind." Lacey clutched the cording from her hatbox and smiled at the stranger. He'd not yet introduced himself. These western men were a rough lot—rough but strong. He'd filled the biggest wheelbarrow she'd ever seen, then hefted her trunk across the handles as if it weighed no more than a pillow. Shoving the heavy burden through the rutted streets didn't even leave him breathless. He'd stayed in the street but next to the boardwalk so she'd not have to contend with the hazardous road any more than necessary.

"Open the door. I'll tote in your belongings."

Lacey rapped on the door to what appeared to be the residential portion of the diner.

"Open it," he ordered as he lumbered up. "Millie's probably knocked out from the laudanum Doc gave her."

"Oh. I see." Though it felt intrusive to barge in, Lacey understood the necessity. "Very well." The door creaked open to reveal a jumbled mess. Lacey yanked the door shut. "If you'd be so kind as to leave the trunk here, I'll drag it inside later."

"You couldn't drag this thing if it were empty. Get the door."

She shook her head. "I'm dreadfully sorry. Truly I am. I'm not trying to be difficult, and I appreciate your strength.

It's just that. . .oh, dear. Well, Aunt Millie's hurt. She simply hasn't felt up to tending to matters."

Her trunk thumped loudly on the boardwalk. The man looked at her like she'd taken leave of her senses. "Suit yourself." He wrapped huge, blackened hands around the handles of his wheelbarrow and trundled back across Ranger Road to the smithy. Suddenly the width of his shoulders and his uncommon strength made perfect sense. Lacey tilted her head to read the sign. JEFFREY WILSON. BLACKSMITH.

"God, please bless Mr. Wilson."

"Which one?" a frail, raspy voice asked from behind her.

Lacey whirled around. From the wild wisps of her gray hair to the tattered hem of her dressing gown and the sling on her arm, the woman looked positively ghastly. "Aunt Millie?"

"In the flesh. Which Mr. Wilson?" She motioned with her good arm for Lacey to enter.

Lacey gripped her hatbox and valise as she stepped over the threshold. She'd never seen a place in such a sad state. Afraid she'd blurt out something hurtful, she grasped at the slim thread of conversation. "How many Mr. Wilsons do you have in this town?"

"Three. The old codger who used to be a ranger, the sheriff, and the blacksmith."

"I see. The blacksmith just escorted me from the train station." She set her valise and hatbox on a nearby table and patted the woman's good hand. "I'm here to help you now."

"Imagine that." Aunt Millie quirked a lopsided smile. "So why don't you tell me who you are?"

The question nearly felled Lacey. Then she recalled the blacksmith mentioning how the doctor gave Aunt Millie laudanum. No wonder the poor dear soul was a bit confused! "I'm Lacey, Tobias's daughter. I've come to help you since you hurt your arm."

The old woman squinted, then bobbed her head. The tortoiseshell comb holding up her wispy gray bun slid lower, and her topknot loosened into a precarious nest of tangles. "I remember you. Last I saw you, you were clinging to your mama's fancy ball gown and missing your front teeth. I see good, sound ones filled right in."

Having her teeth remarked upon as though she were a mare under consideration for purchase stunned Lacey. Then again, poor Aunt Millie dealt with gruff men all day long. No doubt, now that she had feminine companionship, the gentler side of her nature would shine. "How kind of you to remember Mama. I only hold a few memories of her. Perhaps, after you rest, you could share some of your recollections." Lacey took her aunt's arm and led her toward an open doorway. Surely this must lead to the residential portion of the building.

"You hungry, girl?"

"I confess, I am. Perhaps you'd like me to prepare us lunch."

"Then we're headed the right direction." Aunt Millie shuffled ahead and blocked Lacey's view for a moment. When she stepped to the side, pride rang in her voice. "How do you like it?"

A fair-sized kitchen spread before Lacey. Well, she thought it was a kitchen. Pots, pans, kettles, and roasters lay stacked on the stove and counter and hung from the ceiling. Towers of plates listed perilously close to the edge of what she supposed was a sink. Glass canisters formed a jumble in the center of a table, and a cat lazed across the far side of that table, soaking up warmth from a sunbeam. Pretending to ignore the sad state of the room, Lacey pulled off her gloves. "It's plain to see you have a well-equipped establishment. I'll get to work. Is there anything in particular you'd fancy?"

⟨∽⟩

"Jeff."

The hammer clanged down on the horseshoe one last time; then Jeff set the piece back into the fire. "Yeah?"

Two old men hovered by the rail in his smithy. No one

stepped beyond that rail—he'd established that rule straight off, and never once had he regretted it. It kept folks from getting hit by the hammer, sparks, or worse. It also kept them from meddling with him when he worked.

Not that anyone ever managed to keep what the town collectively called "the meddling men" from sticking their noses into other folks' business. Four retired Texas Rangers had founded the town after they'd spent the bulk of their adult years directing and fixing issues and problems. Now, in a peaceful town, the old guys couldn't limit themselves to dallying with dominoes or grumbling over checkers. From their vantage point on the boardwalk, they were worse busybodies than a pack of gossipy widows.

And here two of them were. His uncle Ebenezer leaned forward and cleared his throat. "Pretty filly you were escortin' down the avenue this morning."

Big old Swede nodded his silver-blond head. "Ja. So, what is this? Did you send for a bride?"

"A bride?" Jeff burst out laughing. "Not a chance."

"It's past time you married up," Uncle Eb declared. "Your cousin's happy as a clam now that he married up with Peony."

Mentioning Peony and clams in the same breath seemed daft, but Jeff didn't bother to share his opinion. The less he said, the better off he'd be. Once someone took a mind to challenge the meddling men, the old men took it as a personal affront and reckoned they had to defend their honor by proving themselves right.

"So who is this pretty girl?" Swede asked.

"Millie's kin. Gustavson's mare threw a shoe. I need to get her shod before he comes back."

"Millie's kin, huh?" Swede crammed his thumbs into his belt and rocked to and fro. "Think she can cook any better than Millie?"

"Anyone can cook better than Millie," Eb said in a wry tone.

"No telling," Jeff said gloomily. "Could have inherited Millie's recipes."

All three men sighed. Jeff used his pinchers to pull the horseshoe from the fire and hooked it over the conical end of the anvil, then started pounding it into shape again.

"A man has to have a cast-iron stomach to survive Millie's food. I suppose I'd better keep payin' Lula at the boardin'-house for chow." Swede frowned. "Even my nephew cooks better than that."

Jeff purposefully clanged his hammer extra loud just to drown out their conversation. After all, the two men were directly responsible for matching up his cousin Rafe with

Peony, the dressmaker, last Christmas.

Ever since then, the bachelors in Cut Corners had been manipulated into any number of situations wherein the meddling men tried to match them up with anyone in a skirt.

"Of course he will, won't you, Jeff?" his uncle half shouted.

Jeff knew better than to agree when he hadn't heard what they'd said. He shoved the horseshoe back into the fire and picked up the awl so he could drive holes into the shoe and be done with it. "Don't know what you were jawing over."

Swede harrumphed. "No offense, you understand."

Jeff looked to his uncle for an explanation.

"We were discussing how you've sorta let yourself go. It's the heat and coal and all. . .but I'm sure now that we've called it to your attention, you'll spruce up a bit."

Even though he stood right beside the forge, Jeff's blood ran cold. "I'm not trying to impress anyone."

"Didn't say you had to." His uncle pretended to be interested in a sample brand burned into the wall. "But you'd do well to take your Saturday night bath—"

"And get your hair trimmed," Swede tacked on for good measure.

They were reaching for something to needle him about.

Because of the grime from the smithy, Jeff bathed every day, whether he needed to or not. Why, he probably bought more soap from the mercantile than a family of eight. Instead of saying a thing, he snorted.

"You've been keepin' company too long with horses, son. Snortin' and tossin' your mane like a riled stallion."

"Jay Harris took his shears to me just last week."

"Humph." Swede managed to use that sound to great advantage. Jeff wondered how long it took him to cultivate just the right tone to make it dismissive and disparaging all at the same time. Probably did it for survival's sake, because he had that lilting tonal quality as part of his accent that made him seem more like an affable farmer than a gritty Texas Ranger.

Jeff grabbed nails and stuffed them into the pocket of his leather apron, then slung the horseshoe on the anvil and closed one eye as he measured and punched the holes with a steadiness borne of experience. Done with that, he plunged the shoe into the water bucket and relished the satisfying hiss it produced.

"You men'll have to excuse me." Jeff nodded curtly toward them and headed out the side door to the corral attached to his place.

"Forget about that mare and think about the pretty filly

across the street!" his uncle called.

Jeff scowled. "Why don't you go tell Swede's nephew about her?"

The two old men exchanged a conspiratorial look and hotfooted out of the shop.

Jeff went over to the mare, stooped, and held her leg fast between his knees. In no time at all, she boasted a perfectly fitted shoe.

He straightened up, gave the mare a chunk of carrot, and chuckled. "I ought to feel guilty about sending them to Erik, but it's every man for himself."

"Excuse me, sir."

He tensed at the sound of that soft feminine voice. Silly Boston woman. Exact same words she used early this morning at the train. Was that her standard greeting? Jeff turned. "Yes?"

"Aunt Millie tells me you deliver coal to her. Could I trouble you to bring over more?"

"Sure."

The woman had changed into a simple calico dress, but it looked anything but plain on her. Judging from the damp tendrils corkscrewing around her flushed face, she'd been busy. She smiled—a friendly, sort of shy smile. "Thank you ever so much."

"I'll be by shortly." There. That served as a polite dismissal. It was the best he could manage. She might be pretty as a picture and smell sweeter than a rose garden, but Jeffrey Wilson wasn't looking for a wife, and with Uncle Eb plotting and scheming, the last thing Jeff wanted was to be seen near Millie's niece. He wanted her to go away. The sooner the better.

Chapter 2

Wonderful! Thank you." Lacey stood to one side
as Jeff brought in a full scuttle of coal.

"Don't mention it."

She inched back a bit farther and stood on tiptoe to
swipe a smudge off the wall. "You've been so kind. Would
you care to join us for supper?"

"No."

He answered so quickly, Lacey wondered what she'd said
to offend him. She hid the soiled cleaning rag behind her
back and offered, "Maybe another time."

He hitched his shoulder and headed out the door.

Lacey didn't dwell on his terrible manners. She had too
much to accomplish, and troubling herself over his surly ways

would be a waste of time. She'd dealt with fractious children and found it wisest to ignore such dark moods. Most often, they blew away like a bank of unwelcome thunderclouds. Not that he was at all like the little girls she'd worked with. Mr. Wilson belonged to that mysterious gender with whom she'd rarely interacted. Growing up in a young ladies' academy severely limited her ability to associate with men. To be sure, with his imposing physique, deep voice, and unmistakable strength, Mr. Wilson was the epitome of masculinity.

Still, it would have been nice for him to notice what she'd accomplished.

But he didn't see the place. *I shut the door so he wouldn't know how Aunt Millie let the place fall to rack and ruin. Well, no matter.* Lacey felt the satisfaction of a job well started. Certainly she couldn't consider it well done. Too much remained on her to-do list.

The list lay on the table—the clean, catless table—weighted down with two of the freshly scrubbed canisters. Every last dish, pot, and pan now rested neatly in a hutch, cabinet, or crate. She'd used sink after sink of water and half a cake of soap to wash them all. The windows and floor shone.

So did her nose.

Lacey giggled at herself for that vain thought. No one here in Cut Corners would give a fig for what she looked like or how she behaved. They'd simply be glad Aunt Millie had help and the diner offered decent meals. It would be fun to do this—sort of a holiday. All the other young ladies at the school got to go on trips and vacations, but she'd always remained on the premises. Father never managed to arrange his important business schedule in such a manner as to be home during the school term breaks. Well, this was her vacation. Once Aunt Millie healed, Lacey would pack her trunk and head back to Boston, where a more prestigious school had offered her a very flattering position.

In the meantime, plenty needed doing. Poor Aunt Millie was behind the times. She'd never read Beeton and didn't live according to the all-important maxim that ruled a woman's world. "A place for everything and everything in its place," Lacey quoted as she strove to decide how to make a place for the hundreds of unmatched knives, forks, and spoons she kept unearthing in odd nooks and crannies. So far, she'd resorted to dumping them into three buckets she'd set on a table in the diner.

The diner. She shuddered. The place was a veritable pigsty. No one had come to help clear the tables from the meal Aunt Millie had been serving the day she broke her arm. It had taken every scrap of Lacey's fortitude to collect and scrub those dishes. Bless Aunt Millie's heart, she'd slept through the day thanks to a dose of laudanum. Before the poor old woman woke, Lacey still had several things she wanted to accomplish. If she stayed on the schedule she'd set for herself, Lacey estimated she'd have the diner open for business the day after tomorrow.

⁓

"Excuse me, sir. Could I trouble you to fill this?"

There she goes again. "Excuse me, sir." Her pretty little head must be full of manners and empty of brains. Jeff told himself he wasn't going to turn, but he did. Resplendent in a light purplish dress, Miss Mather handed a list to the grocer. Jeff couldn't decide whether the grocer smiled because of the woman's charm or because the long list would make for a profitable day. Either way, Miss Mather had just made herself a friend in Cut Corners.

"No trouble at all." Lionel Sager beamed at her. "I'll have it done in a trice. I heard tell we had a new lady in town. No one mentioned you were so lovely."

"You're too kind."

The way her thick lashes lowered might well be a practiced response, but Jeff couldn't deny that the fetching blush filling her cheeks was genuine. She acted as if men didn't shower her with compliments all the time. He grew angry with himself for paying any attention and spun back around.

Soap. He'd come to get more soap.

A moment later, Miss Mather stood by his side. A wooden basket was looped over her arm, and she'd already put two cakes of lye soap inside. She stood on tiptoe to look farther back on the display. "Good morning, Mr. Wilson." She helped herself to two more bars of soap—fancy ones. Larkin's Sweet Home and Larkin's Oatmeal Toilet Soap.

"Morning." He grabbed an ordinary bar of Pears.

"It's a pleasure to see Cut Corners boasts such a well-stocked mercantile."

He nodded, then headed toward the counter. Gordon Brooks walked past him, leaving a choking cloud of Hoyt's cologne in his wake. The smirk on the saloon owner's face left nothing to the imagination, and Jeff spun back around. He didn't want his name paired up with Miss Lacey Mather's, but he couldn't leave a poor, defenseless lady to the schemes of a rogue.

"Gordon Brooks at your service." Brooks doffed his hat.

"Thank you," Lacey said as she added knitting needles to her basket, "but the storekeeper has already offered his capable services."

Jeff watched in amusement as she breezed around a corner and busied herself with choosing a ball of string. Brooks followed. "I was merely introducing myself. Here in the untamed regions, a man learns to introduce himself to a lady.

Otherwise, someone else will beat him to her since ladies are so few and far between."

"Sir!" Lacey pressed a hand to her throat and gave him a shocked look. "I saw several God-fearing women as I came down the boardwalk and must protest the slur you've made upon their good character."

"I did say there were a few," Brooks said in a placating tone. "I meant no offense. My intent was merely to make your acquaintance and ask you to supper."

"I'll have to refuse your invitation."

"Why?" Brooks looked flummoxed that his oily charm hadn't worked on her.

"Because I must."

Jeff didn't bother to smother his smile. She actually made that flimsy excuse sound like a reason. He'd thought the little lamb needed to be rescued from the wolf, but that wolf was starting to resemble a whipped puppy. Still, it wouldn't be wise for her to make an enemy of such a man. Jeff cleared his throat. "The lady is being discreet. Fact is, she and her aunt already asked me to supper."

"Yes, yes, we did." She gave Jeff a look of sheer gratitude.

Lionel Sager rounded the corner with a bag on his shoulder. "Miss? This is the last of my sugar. I'll wire for more on the next train, but if you don't mind, I'd like to split the bag so I can keep some stock."

"Please do." She edged farther away from Brooks. "I don't believe I have beans on my list. Do I?"

"Come take a look."

As she walked to the counter, Jeff growled at Brooks, "Leave her alone."

"You Wilsons are all cut from the same cloth—think you run the town." Brooks shook his head. "You got it all wrong. Money is power, and I'm the one in Cut Corners with more of it than most of you put together."

"To my way of thinking, the important things can't be bought."

"Maybe not." Brooks paused, then tacked on, "But that's because those are the things you win." He tugged a pack of poker cards from his vest pocket, then shoved them back down. "Anytime you want, there's room for you in a game."

Jeff grinned. "Sitting at a supper table's my style. Card tables don't hold any appeal."

Vivian Sager approached them. "Pardon me, but I need to get a tin of lard for Miss Mather's order. It's behind you, Mr. Brooks."

Gordon Brooks's suave facade slipped as he scrambled out of Vivian's way. Known for being clumsy, she managed to drop or bump things with disconcerting regularity. He straightened his coat and headed for the door. On his way out, Brooks began to whistle.

"The Girl I Left Behind Me." Vivian identified the tune as she grabbed the bucket of lard. "He'd better not be whistling that about me."

"Allow me." Jeff grabbed the five-gallon tin from her before she crippled one of the two of them by dropping it. He took it to the counter and set it with a rapidly growing pile of groceries.

Lacey stood by the spice display and kept chucking tins into her basket. "Since you're here, Mr. Wilson, perhaps you could tell me if you prefer stewed tomatoes, butter beans, or succotash for supper."

Succotash. He loved succotash. Then again, no use spoiling one of his favorite things by having her massacre it. "Whatever's easiest."

"It's all the same to me."

I'll bet. Just like it is to Millie. How did I rope myself into eating over there tonight?

"I have asparagus," Lionel suggested. "End of the season. Won't be in again until next year."

Jeff shrugged. "I'll leave the menu up to Miss Mather." In all actuality, he hated asparagus. Never did seem quite right, gnawing on something that looked like a bloated, sickly pencil. Then again, he'd be needing bicarbonate after the meal anyway.

Miss Mather set her basket on the counter. The thing overflowed with a crazy collection of luxuries and nonsensical things. Soap, knitting needles, string, paprika, cloves, thyme, tooth powder, and two licorice ropes. "I think this is the last of it."

Vivian scratched off the last thing on the long list and squinted through her thick glasses. "If you think of anything else, you can run back. It's not like Boston where you'd have to take a buggy and need an escort."

"You must enjoy that freedom." Lacey's voice carried a tinge of longing. "It's so refreshing to be here."

"I'll put this on Millie's account." Lionel added the last few items and circled the total.

"Oh no." Miss Mather promptly pulled a small purse from the bottom of the basket and drew out a dozen or more ten-dollar greenbacks.

"Perhaps you'd like to go to the bank and deposit that," Lionel half choked.

"I've already been to the bank," she said blithely.

I had this woman pegged from the start. Daddy has money. That confirmation felt like the last nail in Jeff's coffin. No woman from a wealthy family learned to cook. He silently set a bottle of Peabody's Seltzer on the counter.

Chapter 3

I declare, Aunt Millie, you'd think that man's been starving for a decade," Lacey said as she finished washing the supper dishes. Jeffrey Wilson had come over, asked a nice blessing over the food, then taken very modest portions. After the first few bites, he'd practically inhaled the remainder of the food on his plate and accepted seconds with gusto. . .then taken thirds.

Aunt Millie rested her elbow on the table and propped her head in her hand. "Barely said a word, but his mouth was full."

"So he's usually more talkative?"

"Not much." The cat jumped up into Aunt Millie's lap. "He's got a weakness for critters, though. Talks to horses, dogs, and cats. Isn't that right, Tiger?"

Tiger purred in response.

"Oh, that plate you're washing belongs to Peony Wilson. She brought over some meals for me. I'm surprised she hasn't bustled over to meet you."

Suds splashed everywhere as Lacey dunked the plate. "Don't tell me I asked her husband or brother here for supper and didn't invite her!"

"No, no. She's married to Rafe—the sheriff. He's Jeff's cousin. That's a mighty fancy apron you've got on."

Lacey didn't bother to glance down. She owned four aprons—all of them cut off the same pattern, each with a different floral pattern embroidered across the bodice. "All of the young ladies learn needlework at the academy. This is an everyday one. There's another that's my Sunday-best."

"You'd better plan on wearing mine. Stains'll never come out of that white cotton."

"Madame taught us how to handle each type of spill." Lacey smiled. "But I thank you for your generous offer. What time do you normally serve breakfast?"

"Half past six, I unlock the door. Folks wander in whenever they've a mind to. Wouldn't expect too many to come tomorrow. They won't know the diner's open for business again."

The next morning, Lacey cracked the very last egg she'd bought into the skillet. She'd planned for those eggs to last three days. They hadn't lasted three hours! Aunt Millie tromped into the kitchen and wedged two more plates into the crate beside the sink. "Erik Olson wants another order of flapjacks."

"Another!" Lacey flipped several on the griddle, then shuffled the spatula beneath the egg and slid it onto a plate that held a sizzling slab of ham and handed the plate to her aunt. "I'm out of eggs."

Aunt Millie headed toward the dining room and called over her shoulder, "Not to worry. Just whip up some more flapjacks."

"More flapjacks? But I don't have eggs!" Lacey chased after her. "We'll have to close till lunch."

The entire noisy dining room suddenly went silent. Lacey stood in the doorway and stared at the shocked faces of what looked like the entire population of Cut Corners. Four older gentlemen glowered at her. One thumped his coffee cup on the table. "Can't do that. It's criminal."

"Don't worry," Aunt Millie said. "I told her to just make more flapjacks."

"I don't have eggs to make more batter for—" Lacey shrieked, "The flapjacks!" as she whirled around and ran back to the stove. Half of them were acceptable. The others— She scraped them off and winced.

"Finally got 'em cooked all the way through. I wasn't sayin' anything, but those others looked half-raw to me." Aunt Millie shoved out a plate and set the charred ones aside. "Crispy ones taste the best. 'Specially with apple butter on 'em."

"Bless you," Lacey said softly. Her great-aunt showed great consideration by speaking such kind words when those pancakes were only suitable for—

"Well?" a deep male voice asked. Lacey looked over and started to laugh. Half a dozen men crowded the doorway. She wasn't sure who had asked. "I believe Aunt Millie said Erik Olson ordered flapjacks. He has five coming to him. There are. . ." She took quick inventory and reported, "Seven more left."

"I'll pay a nickel apiece for 'em!"

"I'll pay a dime!"

"I'll wash the dishes," a woman said from the other entry, "if you share your recipe."

Four old gents hunkered over the barrel and pretended to study the checkerboard. Ebenezer Wilson said, "Can't let this one get away."

"Only had breakfast," Stone Creedon muttered. "Don't

know if she can cook anything else yet."

"Who cares? I'll settle for breakfast."

"We must come up with a plan." Chaps reached over and methodically jumped his checker. "King me."

Swede grumbled, "Ja, ja. I king you."

Eb lowered his voice. "Swede, your nephew liked her flapjacks. If we tie her apron strings to a man here in town, that'll make sure she stays at the stove!"

"Erik saw her. Says she's pretty but she talks funny."

No one made mention of Swede's accent. Then again, no one made a comment about Chaps's English accent, either. Stone let out a snarling sound. "He can get used to her accent if he likes her cooking."

"It would be wise to have other gentlemen express interest," Chaps mused. "Nothing makes a woman more attractive than the fact that other men want her."

"Who cares about other men wanting her? The fact that she knows her way around a kitchen is recommendation enough."

"It doesn't matter what we think," Eb Wilson said. "We gotta convince some young buck here in Cut Corners to pay her court."

"Your nephew's a good prospect." Chaps leaned back and smirked at the checkerboard. "He's the first man to see her, and he's already been a supper guest."

"Eb and me, we already tried to convince him." Swede's voice dragged with disappointment. "He isn't interested in her much."

Stone kicked the toe of his scuffed boot against the edge of the boardwalk to dislodge a dirt clod. "Who cares if he don't like her mush? She can cook plenty of other stuff."

Ignoring the fact that his old crony's deafness had him speaking nonsense, Swede announced, "I know what to do."

"What?" Chaps and Eb asked in unison.

"This." Swede leaned forward, took a checker, and hopped it across the entire board like a cricket on desert stones. Scooping up all of Chaps's pieces, he slapped his knee with the other hand and chortled. "You got the king, but I got the game."

"Crazy old coot," Stone muttered. "I thought he figured out something important."

Eb watched as Lacey sashayed down the boardwalk and into the mercantile. Every last bachelor either stared or followed after her. "Fellas, we might not have to do much a'tall. Seems Miss Lacey Mather might need our help to fight off the men instead of us draggin' 'em to her doorstep."

◦◦◦◦

The doors to the diner didn't stop swinging. From the moment the folks in Cut Corners discovered Lacey Mather could cook, they'd beat a path to her door. Morning, noon, and night, she'd dash out with chalk in her hand, write up a menu in the fanciest script ever seen, and run back to her stove. Well—to Millie's stove. Only no one wanted it to be Millie's. They all loved Millie just fine, but her cooking could gag a skunk. Even now, folks could tell what Lacey prepared and what Millie made. Lacey's biscuits rose to fluffy perfection; Millie's would make fine sinkers if someone planned to go fishing. Lacey's batch of gravy could coax a full sentence of praise from grumpy old Stone Creedon; Millie's had lumps big enough to fool a man into thinking he got a dumpling.

Clang, clang, clang. Jeff worked on repairing Heath's plow. He'd sharpen it free of charge. Though it took a little extra time, he always wanted his customers to feel they got a good deal. Besides, he could sit outside the smithy by his large whetstone and watch the parade of swains going to eat at Millie's. The food tasted great, but word around town was the bachelors had more than just a full plate in mind. Many intended to court the pretty little gal. Lacey might think they were claiming their steak; Jeff knew they were staking their claim. There went Harold Myers, hair slicked back and a string tie, and it was just an ordinary Tuesday night. Bay rum wafted clear across the road as Ticks McGee headed into the diner.

Yup, no doubt about it. I've got a front-row seat for first-class entertainment.

"Hey, son." Uncle Ebenezer sauntered over. "Ain't it 'bout time you cooled off, cleaned up, and chowed down?"

"In a while."

"Best you not wait. Miss Mather might run outta grub again." Uncle Eb's head jutted forward as he imparted, "Happens 'least once a day."

Jeff jabbed his thumb back toward the forge. "Beans already on the fire."

"You're fixin' to eat your own cooking?" Eb shook his head. "Heat from that forge must be fryin' your brain."

"You taught me how to make 'em," Jeff replied. "They've been good enough all these years."

"Son, when you ain't got nuthin' but a mule to ride, you ride it. Only a fool keeps on a-riding that flea-bitten old beast when someone offers him a high-steppin' filly."

"You're assuming I aim to go somewhere. I'm happy to stay put."

❧

"I'm flattered, sir, but I simply cannot." Lacey refilled Ticks McGee's coffee mug and moved on down the table, topping off the mugs.

"Why not?" Mr. McGee demanded. "You'd never want

for nothing. I'd treat you real good. My job at the telegraph even comes with the upstairs rooms for us."

Everyone in the diner awaited her answer. Lacey hadn't realized the men were being more than friendly until Ticks just proposed to her in front of everyone. She'd thought the gangly telegraph operator had been joking. He wasn't. *"Men are fragile creatures—their pride is easily damaged."* Madame's words echoed in her mind. Lacey set down the big blue enamel coffeepot and gifted Ticks with a gentle smile. "You've honored me with your offer, sir. Truly, I'm flattered, but I cannot accept because I'm set to take a position at Le Petite Femme Academie once my aunt is better."

Angry roars and denials ripped through the diner.

"The matter is settled." She headed toward the kitchen for refuge.

"What was all that noise?" Aunt Millie asked as she sat at the table and made another bowl of coleslaw. "And where's the salt?"

Lacey scooted a cup toward her aunt. "Here. I measured this out for you already." The fact that the cup held sugar instead of salt—well, Lacey had to do something. Aunt Millie seemed to have very. . .unique notions about her recipes. Rather than offend her aunt, Lacey simply started supplying bowls with already measured dry ingredients so her aunt could still be helpful. So far, the solution had worked wonderfully.

"How about adding a little kick to this with some chili powder?" Aunt Millie asked after adding the sugar and taking a taste.

Chili powder in coleslaw? Public marriage proposals from near strangers? Lacey shook her head in disbelief.

"No?" Aunt Millie looked disappointed.

"Raisins. They'll complement the pork roast, don't you think?" Lacey swiped the chili powder from the spice rack and slipped it into her apron pocket. No use leaving temptation on hand. "You've made a wonderful suggestion, though. We could make chili and corn bread for lunch tomorrow."

Mollified, Aunt Millie dumped raisins into the coleslaw. "Best you get plenty of peppers from Sager's. These men are Texans. They like their chili hot."

Aunt Millie's idea of hot would no doubt have every last man in Cut Corners on his knees, praying for redemption. With that concern in mind, Lacey hovered over the stove the next day. Jeff Wilson lumbered in with more coal. As he filled the box and added more coal to the stove for her, he sniffed. "What is that?"

"Chili." She smiled at him and tapped the edge of the

enormous pot on her left. "This one is regular. The other is hot."

"Hmm." He washed off at the pump, dried his hands, and swiped a spoon. After taking a taste of the hot pot, he gave her a patient look. "Miss Mather, back in Boston you fix beans with brown sugar and molasses. That's all well and good, but you're in Texas."

"Why, of course I am."

"Texas chili doesn't use beans—but just this once, we'll overlook that."

Another peculiar thing about Texas. At least he was nice about telling me. And the chili tastes perfectly fine the way it is.

"The real problem is, that stuff's milder than kissin' your sister." Jeff grabbed a bottle of Tabasco and upended it over the pot. "Millie, head on over to the mercantile. Grab up half a dozen more bottles, a mess of peppers, and grab me a ginger ale while you're at it."

"Sure thing!" Aunt Millie shot Lacey an I-told-you-so look and rushed out the door.

Horrified at how he blithely spoiled a perfectly decent pot of chili, Lacey spluttered. Just the fumes from the Tabasco had her gasping for air.

"Now that she's gone," Jeff said, continuing to give the bottle emphatic shakes to empty it, "I'm going to talk turkey.

Your aunt's a fine woman, but she's a miserable cook. I heard tell you plan to leave once she gets better. Take pity on us all and teach her your recipes, will you?"

Staring at the pot in utter dismay, Lacey said, "You seem to share her chili recipe."

"Simple rule: In Texas, you make the chili so it blows off the top of your head when you take a taste." He grinned. "Then you triple the hot stuff." He gawked at the spice rack. "Where's the chili powder?"

Lacey pulled it from her apron pocket. "I had to hide it from Aunt Millie so she wouldn't put it in the coleslaw last night."

His features looked pained. "So that's what she does to it." He dumped an eye-popping amount into the first pot, then as much into the second, and finally set down the tin. "At least she won't be able to do it again until you buy more."

"You emptied the chili powder and Tabasco into it!"

"Yup." He stirred the pot.

Aunt Millie returned so fast, Lacey suspected she'd already sent word to the mercantile to have everything ready. Lacey couldn't even cut more peppers. Her eyes, nose, and fingers already stung. Jeff grabbed a knife, hacked the peppers into an unsightly mess, and dumped them into the chili as Aunt Millie merrily shook Tabasco into the second pot.

Lacey put another pan of corn bread into the oven and wondered how she'd ever explain to the hungry patrons that the main dish had been spoiled.

Jeff tilted his head toward the icebox. "Now get yourself some milk."

"Would you care for a glass?"

"Don't need it." He waited until she had a glassful. "Now taste this."

Lacey didn't want to sample it. Then again, she didn't want to be rude. At least he didn't have a lot on the spoon. She opened her mouth.

Chapter 4

"Oh. Ohh." Lacey's hand went up to her mouth. The strangled sound coming out of her made Jeff drop the spoon and grab the milk from her.

"Here. Drink." He lifted the glass and tried to peel her hand from her mouth. Her big hazel eyes filled with tears that overflowed and spilled down her cheeks.

"It'll help. Drink!"

Both of her hands clamped around his. The poor woman could scarcely breathe, but she took a sip and fought to swallow.

"Drink it all. Fast." Jeff hadn't ever seen such a pitiful sight. Proper little Lacey Mather broke out into a full-on sweat, and her face rivaled a tomato for color. Tears poured down her face, and she kept making a sound of pure anguish.

"Wa—" She tried to scramble away. "Wa. Ur."

"Oh no. No water!" Millie stood in front of the pump by the sink.

"More milk." Jeff sloshed milk into the glass and shoved it back at Lacey. "Milk cools the fire." She couldn't decide what to do or where to go, so he yanked out a chair and shoved her into it. As she drank the milk, Millie flapped a dish towel to cool her off.

"I gave her a taste out of the milder pot," he said to Millie.

Lacey said something—it sounded sort of like "murder," but he wasn't sure. Maybe it was "mother."

"Millie, let's have her lie down." Jeff half lifted Lacey from the chair. She clutched the milk bottle for dear life. "Yeah, princess. You bring that along."

With Millie as chaperone, it would be decent enough for him to escort Lacey back to the bedchamber, only Lacey didn't cooperate. They'd scarcely gotten into the parlor when she pulled away and sank onto the horsehair settee and gulped more milk—directly from the bottle.

"She can't breathe," Millie said as she shoved at his shoulder. "You go on back and stir the pot."

Jeff took his cue and left. Women and their stays. Once

Millie loosened Lacey, then she ought to improve. Or so he hoped. He stirred the pots, tasted each, and couldn't fathom why she'd reacted at all. They were still blander than rattlesnake. Well, Lacey wouldn't try another taste, so he might as well go ahead and finish seasoning the pots so they'd be ready for the lunch crowd. She'd done fine with the garlic and onion, but the woman didn't have a hint on how much zing and heat to add. Satisfied he'd salvaged lunch, Jeff decided he'd better try to rescue the fair maiden.

"How's she doing, Millie?"

"Hot," Lacey croaked.

Jeff tore open the icebox and chipped out a chunk of ice. His bandanna wasn't exactly clean, but it would have to do. He wrapped the ice in it and ventured back into the parlor. Ever since she'd arrived, the woman always looked like a page straight out of that *Godey's Lady's Book* his aunt used to pore over. Not any longer. Hair askew, clothing loosened, and apron off, Lacey looked like she'd been dragged through a knothole backward. The sight of her melted his heart.

"Ice." He slid it across her forehead. "Millie, I'll just put the pots on the table and let folks serve themselves today. Why don't you put the corn bread out?"

Lacey grabbed his wrist. "No. Dumb. Keyhole."

"Princess, I'm not going to dump it out. It won't kill

HERE COOKS THE BRIDE

anybody." The accusation in her eyes had him squirming. "Just drink a little more milk. Trust me."

Her pretty round jaw dropped open in shock, then clamped shut. Jeff figured it was a good thing she couldn't talk much right now.

⟨≈⟩

Lacey stood in church and held the hymnal, but she didn't sing. Couldn't sing. Ever since yesterday's chili debacle, her tongue and throat belonged to a dragon. A whole day now. An entire day of not being able to speak much, taste at all, or sing a note. And the men! Every last bachelor in town— except Jeffrey Wilson—wouldn't leave her alone. They'd tasted that pot of bubbling brimstone, declared it the best they'd ever eaten, and vowed they'd never let her leave Cut Corners. Unable to deny any responsibility for that vile dish, she'd become a celebrity.

Jeff Wilson—that rascal—didn't let on. No, he didn't. Neither did Aunt Millie.

Both of them ought to visit the altar and confess their dirty deeds.

Only staying mad didn't make sense. Truly this group was a lot of fun. They managed to find the good in just about anything. The fact that they'd eaten every last bit of that dreadful chili proved her point! But they helped one another out. Peony Wilson had come to the diner the first morning it was open and helped wash all of the dishes. Vivian Sager dropped by each morning to see if Lacey needed anything from the mercantile. The old gents who whiled away their days on the boardwalk playing games all kept watch on the children as they darted across the road on their way to and from school. Jeff brought over coal and sharpened her knives. Aunt Millie, for having a painful arm, still kept a cheerful attitude and did her best to help.

When the last chord on the piano died out, Lacey sat down between Aunt Millie and Peony on the bench. Rafe had gotten called to go check something and worried about his wife, so he'd brought her by to "help" get Aunt Millie ready for church. One glance told Lacey why he'd fretted so. Peony alternated between blanching and taking on a peculiar green tint. No wonder Rafe started showing up for breakfast at the diner! Her new friend deserved to reveal the wonderful news when she took a mind to—and not a moment earlier. That being the case, Lacey opened her silk fan and managed to waft it more toward Peony as the parson approached the pulpit.

"We are all part of the family of God," Parson Clune said. "Working together for the betterment of one another and to promote the kingdom of God."

Aunt Millie reached over with her good hand to give Lacey's leg a loving pat. Ever since Mama had passed on and Father had sent her to the academy, Lacey hadn't been part of a family. She didn't have anybody. Well—back in Boston, she didn't. Here, she had Aunt Millie. If it hadn't been for Father's housekeeper sending the telegraph message on to Lacey, she wouldn't have known her great-aunt still lived.

"Instead of considering it a duty to help our brothers and sisters, it is a privilege and honor to serve them in the name of Christ. Christ displayed an attitude of humility by washing the disciples' feet. You can't get any more down-to-earth than that."

Folks in the congregation caught the pun and chuckled.

Parson Clune smiled and continued, "We want to be like the Savior. That means caring for each other in the everyday, mundane, little matters. . . ."

As the sermon continued, Rafe arrived. He scooted onto the bench next to his wife and slid his arm behind her. She immediately leaned into him and relaxed.

"A lady sits upright at all times. Back straight. No slump-ing. Only a lazy woman rests against the back of her chair. . . ." Madame's lessons darted through Lacey's mind, and for the first time they all seemed petty and nonsensical. Rafe cher-ished his wife, and she wasn't feeling her best. To support

her back while she sat on this hard old bench was—well, it was an act of everyday love. It's like in the fairy tales. A happily-ever-after kind of love. *And they're going to have a family.*

After the service, Lacey couldn't get that image out of her mind. Something tugged at her—a longing she couldn't escape. How wonderful it would be to have someone to love and to be loved by! Oh, if she wanted to, she could accept the very next marriage proposal and become a wife within a week. Men asked for her hand with stunning regularity. *But none of them love me, and I don't love them. I can't live day in and day out when there's no love beneath the roof.*

But a small voice inside taunted, *You already have—all your life at the academy.*

Lacey shoved that thought aside. It was untrue. The younger girls flocked to her, and she adored them. And she admired Madame. If anything, the sermon opened her eyes. She could love in Christ's name and by His example in dozens of tiny ways each day. But that plan didn't take away the odd feeling that she was missing out on finding her own happily-ever-after.

Chapter 5

"H oo–oo–ey!" Jeff finished filling the coal bin, took out his bandanna, and flapped it in the air. "Now that you can fire up the stove, I'll open the door and air out this place."

Millie winked. "Long as I've been here—and I'm one of the founding folks of Cut Corners—Ticks McGee never put on any airs for me."

"Put on airs!" Jeff hooted. He opened the door and fanned it back and forth to dispel the overwhelming scent the telegrapher had left in his wake. "The man did a back-stroke through bay rum to deliver that telegram."

"Oh, stop that." Lacey continued to peel potatoes, but laughter tinged her voice.

"I don't dare." Jeff kept fanning the room. "If this place isn't aired out by supper, folks'll all think you got a polecat under the planks."

"Not with all the flowers," Millie said in a droll voice as she stood on tiptoe over at the spice rack. "I'm flat running out of jars for 'em."

"They look pretty on the tables," Lacey said as she set aside a potato, got up, and smoothly took the tin of spice from her aunt. "I'd like to save these cloves for the ham, Aunt Millie. I hope you don't mind."

Millie frowned. "Then what're you going to put on the roast beef?"

"I was thinking maybe we ought to do something together. Madame taught us to mix spices and jar them so we'd have ready-made seasonings specifically for chicken, pork, fish, or beef. It saves a lot of time. After I leave, it'll simplify things for you."

"Great idea!" Jeff beamed at her. "Tell you what: I was fixin' to go to the mercantile to get a few things. I'll bring back some of those nifty Ball-Mason jars. What spices do you need?"

"I'll make a list. We can write the recipes down, too." Lacey smiled at her aunt. "And you can be sure to give me your cowboy cookie recipe and that sweet cornmeal mush.

The girls at the academy will love it."

Jeff grinned at her. Lacey Mather exhibited more tact than anyone he'd ever known. She hadn't even spoken a cross word when Jay Harris and one of the Baxter boys both brought in goldenrod and had everyone in the diner sneezing all day. Men kept bringing her posies, and she'd have her aunt stick them in jars on the dining tables—along with everyone else's. That way, according to Lacey, everyone could enjoy the beauty of Texas. Far as all those men were concerned, Lacey was the Beauty of Texas. But Beauty never once showed the least bit of interest in any of the men.

Millie and Peony did a fair job of sitting on either side of Lacey at worship services; otherwise, a passel of lovesick cowboys all practically trampled the poor woman in hopes of having the honor of sitting by her side. Ticks McGee actually knocked over a bench in church in his rush to be near her.

That wasn't all. She'd befriended the women in town, and even old sourpuss Lula Chamberlain sang her praises. Youngsters were crazy about her, too. Why, she'd taken to baking cookies only the children were offered if they'd finished their meal. Folks in town speculated on how good they must be, and the kids practically licked their plates clean to earn one—but Lacey didn't let the adults have 'em. She declared it as a rule.

Only she'd set one on the ledge by the coal box for Jeff each time he made a delivery. A special one—extra big. Continuing to fan the door, he bit into the cookie. "Mmm."

"I've been meaning to speak with you about increasing the delivery of coal to every other day."

Jeff took another bite and waggled his brows. Mouth full of incredible taste, he suggested, "How about every day?"

Her gaze went from the remains of the cookie to his eyes, then back. "I wouldn't want to cast aspersions on your character or motives. Shall I presume the offer stems from the fact that winter is almost upon us?"

"Miss Mather." Jeff tucked the last portion of the cookie in his mouth, chewed and swallowed it with relish, then grinned. "I wouldn't take offense if you assumed my offer had anything to do with a tasty fringe benefit. No man in his right mind would pass up an opportunity to eat your cooking. As for winter—well, the weather's getting snappy."

She opened the cookie jar and held it out to him. "I've been thinking about that. Perhaps it's time to place an order with Sanger's so the diner isn't without necessities. When do we expect the first snowfall?"

"Snow?" Millie let out a cackle and grabbed a cookie.

Jeff helped himself. "More often than not, it doesn't snow here until late, if at all."

A stricken expression crossed Lacey's pretty face. "You don't have snow for Christmas?"

"A few times we have." It hadn't ever mattered to him, but clearly the thought rocked Miss Mather to the core.

Millie dusted a cookie crumb from her lips. "A bigger mess you've never seen. Folks tracked slush and mud in here and never gave me a moment's rest. All they wanted was coffee, soup, and pie. Can't make much of a profit on that."

"With all the rain we've been getting, I thought—" Lacey let out a small self-conscious laugh. "I suppose it doesn't matter. You're both happy without the snow, and I'll be back in Boston up to my boots in snow for Christmas."

Suddenly the cookie tasted like sawdust. Jeff looked at Lacey and couldn't imagine her leaving. "You don't have to go."

Her eyes widened and glistened with sincerity. "But of course I shall. I've given my word."

&

"Frankly, I don't like the looks of this." Dr. Winston supported Aunt Millie's arm and carefully moved it. "It's healing more slowly than I'd hoped."

"Don't tell me you're going to splint me up again. I won't have it."

Lacey took corn bread from the oven and popped in pans

of chocolate cake. "What do you recommend, Doctor?"

"Not another splint." Aunt Millie's repressive tone matched her taut face.

"If we keep it heavily bandaged and in a sling, that ought to provide enough protection. You cannot use the arm yet for anything. Even lifting the lightest object might well snap the bone again."

"I don't need to be mollycoddled. Using the arm will strengthen it."

Doc folded his arms across his chest. "Millie, you're old, you're stubborn, and you're wrong."

"Two out of those three aren't flaws," she shot back.

"But that still means the doctor needs to bind up your arm," Lacey said.

"Not till after I eat a chunk of that corn bread. Doc, have a seat."

Lacey smiled at the physician. He'd about hit his limit in dealing with her aunt. "Please do sit down. Would you rather have vegetable barley soup or potato cheese?"

"Have the potato cheese. She wouldn't listen to me and add cinnamon or nutmeg to the vegetable barley." Aunt Millie shot Lacey a disgruntled look. "Everyone knows you add nutmeg and cinnamon to things with grains in them."

The doctor choked, coughed, then rasped, "I'd like the

vegetable, please. And Miss Mather, you cannot possibly leave yet. At this point, your aunt still needs your assistance."

"I suspected as much. I'll send a telegram today." The thought of staying in Cut Corners awhile longer filled her with happiness.

The happiness lasted all through serving lunch, clear until she approached the telegraph office. Facing Ticks McGee after she'd turned down his marriage proposal qualified as more than a little awkward. In the time she'd been in Texas, there hadn't been a single day during which she hadn't received a gentleman's offer to take her out for a walk. . .and more than a few had actually embellished the invitation clear into a proposal that she walk down the aisle to him! Once she'd informed the populace that she'd be returning to Boston, Lacey presumed the nonsense would stop. On the contrary, it only got worse.

That scamp Jeff Wilson seemed to find the whole thing hilarious. Indeed, Lacey supposed it was. She tried to keep a sense of perspective. These men were lonely. And hungry. Madame said a man who had a full plate and a quiet woman who listened to him was a happy man. These men were seeking happiness. She oughtn't fault them for following their nature. Lacey just wished their nature would lead them to some other woman.

"Well, well! Miss Mather, what can I do for you?" Ticks perked up.

"Good afternoon, Mr. McGee. I'd like to send a telegram." She'd already composed it back at the diner, so she took the paper from her reticule and handed it across the counter.

"This is quite a lengthy one." He pulled the pencil from behind his ear and dabbed the lead on his tongue. "We could shave it down and save you a bundle."

Lacey suppressed a shudder at the fact that his hair oil slicked the pencil. "I appreciate the offer, sir, but that isn't necessary."

His brows scrunched into a deep V. "It costs a nickel per three words, Miss Mather."

"Yes, I know." She smiled. "I counted it at a hundred fifty-nine words. According to my arithmetic, it should total two dollars and sixty-five cents."

He tapped his pencil against her paper. "It goes against my grain to take advantage of a lady. I'm sure I can help you out. You can't squander your money like that."

"My finances are not your concern, sir. The matter is important, and I'd appreciate you taking the utmost care in transmitting the letter precisely as I composed it." She set the exact cost of the telegram on the counter.

Muttering to himself, Ticks went over to the telegraph

key. He settled into the oak chair, poised his finger over the apparatus, then squinted at the missive. His head shot up. "You're staying?"

"Only for a while longer."

"Why don't you have a seat? You can wait for a reply."

The last thing she wanted to do was spend more time in the stuffy office with a man far too eager to drag her to the altar. "Forgive me for asking you to deliver any reply to the diner. I have a few errands to run."

Exiting the office, she headed for Sanger's Mercantile. Perhaps if she and Vivian looked at what was in stock, they could concoct a softer, more comfortable bandage and sling for Aunt Millie.

Dear Aunt Millie. Lacey fretted over what to do about her relative. The old woman had plenty of spirit and a heart as big as the sky, but there didn't seem to be any reason behind some of her actions. *I'm sure it's the laudanum that makes her forgetful,* Lacey told herself. Then again, Chaps Smythe called her an "odd duck." The appellation did fit—after all, who else would think a roast beef ought to be topped with sugar? Well, regardless, Lacey loved her great-aunt. She wasn't in the least bit upset about extending her stay. What would Jeffrey Wilson say about it, though?

"Are you okay?" Jeff hovered in the doorway.

"Depends on who you're asking." Millie gave him a jaded look as she shuffled across the floor. "I say I'm fine. Doc still wants me trussed up like a coast-to-coast parcel."

He hadn't come to check on Millie's arm, but Jeff nodded. "You do what he wants. We need you completely healed."

"Yes, we do." Lacey stood by the sink dabbing peroxide onto a wad of cotton.

Jeff crossed over toward her and grabbed hold of her hand. Studying her slender fingers, he asked, "Did you cut yourself?" He'd heard she'd bought peroxide at the mercantile, and he'd hotfooted it over here to be sure she was all right. He'd heard other news about Lacey, too, that he wanted to confirm.

"No. I got some drippings on myself when I put the roast in the oven. Peroxide removes bloodstains." She slid her hand loose and continued to fiddle with the front of her too-fancy-for-the-wilds-of-Texas apron. What call did a woman have wearing anything that pristine and frilly when she stood in front of a stove?

"All those facts are a waste, what with you living at that school." Millie dumped sugar into her coffee and shook the spoon at Lacey. "Those girls won't use that knowledge a lick.

They'll marry rich men and have maids and cooks to do the work for 'em."

He saw hurt darken Lacey's eyes. Clearly she felt she'd found what God intended her to do with her life. Having others disparage it upset her. Though he agreed with Millie's assessment, Jeff couldn't bring himself to say so aloud. Instead, he teased lightly, "According to Ticks, the girls will have to make do without you for some time yet."

Lacey nodded. "I'll be staying until just before Christmas. That'll give Aunt Millie plenty of time to heal."

"I think I'll buy another fireplace poker from you, Jeff." Millie winced as she placed her arm on the table. "I'll use it to prod Ticks out of here. The man's making a pest of himself."

"Your niece has been good for business, Millie."

"Amazing what a pretty face'll do." Millie nodded. "Brings 'em all in, and they don't seem to mind that the food's seasoned all wrong. The girl cooks like an easterner."

"I've been able to thank God with a clear conscience for every last meal she's cooked."

Millie gave him a worldly-wise look. "Ecclesiastes 2:24: 'There is nothing better for a man, than that he should eat and drink, and that he should make his soul enjoy good in his labour. This also I saw, that it was from the hand of

God.' That's you, Jeff Wilson. You're happy just to have a full belly and a hot forge."

"Contentment is a fine quality," Lacey said quietly. "Jeff works hard, and his heart belongs to God. In my estimation, that's more than admirable." She turned back to trying to remove the blot on her apron.

Jeff appreciated her compliment. Lacey wasn't one to pass out flattery. He patted the edge of her apron. "Well, you need to take a little credit for that contentment. I'm doing all of my eating here these days."

"You're always most welcome," Lacey said.

Most welcome. Was that just polite banter, or did she mean I'm more welcome than anyone else?

⊰⊱

Peony took a sip of tea and gave Lacey a grateful smile. "It's helping. Thank you."

"Lemon's supposed to help, too. Here. I made lemon spritz cookies for you." Lacey urged her friend to nibble. For the past week and a half, she'd been bringing little meals and treats to tempt Peony. Rafe took all his meals at the diner, and from the lines creasing his face, Lacey knew he was beside himself with worry.

"Dr. Winston says my tummy will settle down in another few weeks."

"Of course it will." Lacey smiled brightly. "In the meantime, since you don't have to worry about cooking, we need to plan your wardrobe for the *accouchement*."

Peony smiled. "Your propriety is so charming. How wonderful to grow up with such refinement."

Lacey urged her to nibble on a second cookie. "I'd scarcely call a school full of chattering girls refined. We were trained in all matters of conduct, but there weren't many opportunities to actually put the lessons into practice."

"I grew up with women, too—but not ones of respectability."

Reaching out, Lacey covered Peony's hand with hers. "Do you think such a thing matters to me? We have no say about the circumstances we're born into. It's what we do with ourselves that matters."

"I felt it only right to confess it. There are those who cannot—"

"Pardon me for interrupting you, Peony, but I cannot abide those with narrow minds and even narrower hearts. From the moment you stepped foot into the diner and offered to help wash up the breakfast dishes, you showed your true heart. God sent you to me as a friend, and I'm thankful. So now that we've settled that, why don't we design a dress for you to wear through Christmas? I'm sure with your clever sewing we could take deep seams to let out as your delicate condition progresses."

"I did order a length of beautiful green paisley."

Once she'd made sure Peony had finished the tea, cookies, and cheese, Lacey headed back to the diner. Aunt Millie was supposed to be placing an order over at Sanger's, and they'd already prepared the chicken pasties. Lacey would start popping them into the oven and have them ready just in time for the lunch crowd. She turned the corner and saw smoke billowing out of the diner window.

Chapter 6

"Well!" Millie plopped down in the chair and fanned herself with a damp, charred dishcloth.

Jeff stamped on another ember and poured one last bucket of water down the wall. The entire window frame looked like a chunk of charcoal, the panes were cracked, and what had once been curtains now made a sad pile of ashes on the floor.

"Aunt Millie!" Lacey barreled into the room.

"Over here. No use fussing."

"Are you well? Did either of you get burned?" Lacey's voice quavered as she made her way to her aunt.

"Wasn't nothing much. No real harm done." Millie shrugged. " 'Cept a couple of the pastries for lunch are singed."

"No one cares about that, Millie. We're just glad you didn't get hurt." Jeff set down the water bucket.

Lacey watched him solemnly. Her hazel eyes reflected a mix of horror and gratitude. One glance at the place told just how close this had come to being a disaster. "Thank you." She stumbled toward the other door and opened it wide. Smoke drafted on the breeze from the first door to the second.

"Smoke follows beauty." Jeff didn't intend to speak aloud. Once he realized he'd done so, he crooked her a grin. "I don't think there's much damage here. Nothing a little sanding, a few replacement boards, and glass won't solve."

"Erik Olson can handle that." Millie leaned back in her chair.

"I'll see him about it after lunch." Lacey stepped through the water puddles on the floor and opened the oven door.

"Careful!" Jeff cinched his arm about her waist and lifted her up and back. He'd barely managed in time. Gray water with gritty bits of soot and coal spilled from the appliance and splattered on the floor.

"Oh my."

Oh my. Jeff wanted to echo Lacey's words—but for an entirely different reason. He'd just grabbed an armful of woman, and he hadn't anticipated the effect. He didn't want to put her down. The sweet scent of her perfume engulfed him.

"The oven's stone-cold."

"Yep." He didn't tell her it took eight buckets of water before the dumb thing stopped steaming—all of course, after the half dozen he'd used on the wall and window. At the moment, he doubted she would accept that information with much poise.

Patting his arm, Lacey said, "You did a wonderful thing, Mr. Wilson. Heroic. There's no doubt you rescued my aunt and the diner."

From the way she twisted, he knew she wanted to be put down. Jeff took a few long strides and grudgingly set her on the dry patch of planks on the far side of the table. "I just happened along."

"Thank the Lord!" Lacey cast a glance at the shelves of towel-covered sheets. "You've already done so much. I do hate to impose, but would you mind awfully if I used your forge?"

"My forge?"

Twenty minutes later, Jeff stood beside Lacey at his forge. The crazy woman was dressed in her calico dress and a frilly white apron; she held a potholder in one slender hand and a long pair of tongs in the other. She'd dug out the biggest pot in the diner, given it to him, and now had lard melted and bubbling in it. "I'd far rather bake these. It's much more healthful," she said as she snagged the chicken pasties from the pot and replaced them with more.

"Smells great."

"Hey, there." Uncle Eb stood over at the rail. He shot Jeff a wily grin. "What's happening here?"

"Your nephew is saving the day." Lacey flashed Uncle Eb a smile. "He put out a fire at the diner, and he's letting me fix lunch here."

"What say, folks just drop by here to pick up their lunch? Looks like they can carry them meat pies."

"I don't know...." Lacey looked up at Jeff. "What do you think?"

"After all the rain, it's a fair day. Ground's dry. We can stick out a bucket of apples and call it a picnic lunch."

"A picnic!" Her face lit up. "Oh, I love picnics. I know just what to do."

By the time lunch was scheduled, Jeff stood back and shook his head at the event. At Lacey's urging, he'd set out a pair of sawhorses and stretched a few solid planks across them. She'd covered them with a red-checkered tablecloth from the diner. A big vat of potato salad, a dish of pickle spears, slices of buttered bread, and a bucket of apples sat along it. Six more tablecloths lay on the ground, weighted by rocks and each holding one of the jars of flowers from the diner. She stepped back and sighed. "If only we had some music!"

"You could sing."

She turned the exact color red as the checkers in the tablecloth. "I'd scare away the diners. I confess, I cannot sing at all."

"No?" Her admission caught him off guard. "I thought those fancy girl schools turned you out with all sorts of musical accomplishments."

"They're supposed to. I failed abysmally. The music master despaired of teaching me to sing. I'm utterly and completely tone deaf. Even worse, I developed the revolting habit of getting hiccups whenever I attempted the flute." Her smile turned charmingly winsome. "It produces the oddest sounds."

"But you played the piano last week at church."

"Only because the pastor implored me to since no one else was more capable. I'm afraid the piano master pronounced my playing 'somewhere between painful and passable.'"

He scowled. "Was everyone there that cruel? I thought they pampered you at those places."

"Honesty is the best policy. How could I work on my shortcomings if no one pointed out the flaws? I do, however, hope to mention my impressions with a bit more tact when I'm overseeing the girls at my next post."

Her next post. She said it so blithely. What did she think she was doing, leaving a dotty aunt and a town full of people who cared for her, just to go back to an institution where truth wasn't tempered with compassion? Jeff wanted to roar. He wanted to rattle some sense into her. No way was he going to let her go.

Chapter 7

Erik Olson pounded in one last nail, then stood back to survey the repairs. "Ja. The window, bigger is nice."

"You outdid yourself," Aunt Millie declared. "I think the man deserves a cookie, don't you, Lacey?"

Lacey nodded. She didn't dare actually open her mouth to reply for fear that she'd start to giggle. The Swedish carpenter had been casting longing looks at the cookie jar from the moment he came over to assess the damage. To his credit, even when he'd been alone in the kitchen, he'd never sneaked a single crumb. His sense of honor touched Lacey. Then again, it didn't exactly surprise her. Erik was Jeff's friend—and as she'd been taught, a man could be judged by the company he kept.

"My niece made you a whole dozen of your own, Erik. You go ahead and enjoy 'em—every last one." Aunt Millie scooted a plate across the table.

Erik grinned and pulled out a chair. "Then I will eat them here. My uncle and the other old men—they will gobble up the plate if I go outside."

"Milk, or coffee?" Lacey offered.

"Both." The carpenter gave her a boyish grin. "Milk for to dunk the cookies. Coffee to remind me I am no longer a boy, even though I enjoy the treat you keep for the children."

Lacey set the beverages before him, then turned back to the oven. She opened the door and pulled out the roaster just long enough to dump in the carrots and potatoes.

"Mmm, mmm, mmm. Something smells great."

She didn't even turn around. "Is there anything you don't like, Jeff?"

"Cranberries." His boots rang across the planks, and coal shuffled into the bin.

"Asparagus. He does not like that, either." Erik grinned. "He calls it 'ugly pencils.' "

Lacey wheeled around. "And I served you asparagus the first time you ate here!"

"Your asparagus is good. Millie, I still think you need to teach her chili doesn't take beans."

The older woman sighed theatrically. "You can lead a horse to water. . . ."

"Aunt Millie! Are you comparing me to a horse?"

"Don't get all het up and scandalized." Aunt Millie's face puckered. "Horses are fine creatures. Loyal. Hardworking."

Jeff shot a look at the new window ledge. "Good work, Erik."

"Thank you."

Lacey took the hint. She grabbed the cookie jar and held it out to him. He looked down at his sooty hands. "Here." Fishing out a pair of cookies, she slipped them into his hands.

"Much obliged." Jeff cast a look at Erik, who was plowing through the plate of cookies like a starving man. "If the old rangers catch wind of you eating those all by yourself, your days are numbered."

"You do not tell them. I will not tell them you eat a cookie each time you come to deliver coal." Erik bit off another chunk. "This is a good bargain. You come out better."

Jeff pounded his friend on the shoulder and belted out a chuckle.

The male camaraderie astonished Lacey. She'd never had an opportunity to watch men interact. The whole time Erik worked, Jeff had tracked in and out, lent a hand, and silently left. Neither of them ever said a word about the assistance.

Rafe Wilson was the same way. He and Jeff were cousins, and they often seemed to carry on entire conversations over the dining table without saying more than a cryptic one- or two-word phrase apiece, grunt, nod, and grin.

Those masculine grins—Jeff's in particular—were oddly gratifying sights. Men, for being such odd, rough creatures, never looked very approachable. But when Jeff's mouth kicked up and his eyes sparkled with laughter, an odd sense of contentment washed over Lacey. Longing to keep him smiling, she said, "I've been thinking about Thanksgiving."

"Diner's closed Thanksgiving and Christmas. I made that mistake the first year. Worked myself silly, and all because everyone else was too lazy. Since then, I have a free pot roast luncheon for all the bachelors on Christmas Eve Day. That's as good as it's gonna get." Aunt Millie rapped the knuckles of her left hand on the table. "Let each of 'em cook their own turkey or goose."

"My goose is cooked, all right," Jeff muttered. He scowled. "Come on, Millie. It's stupid for me to make a whole turkey just for myself."

"You got an uncle and a cousin and his wife. Your family'll take you in."

Lacey inhaled sharply. "Oh, but Peony can't cook. It's too hard for her."

"Good." Jeff's smile looked downright smug. "Then we'll all show up. You name the time."

"Ja, name the time." Erik bobbed his head.

"If you come, Swede will tag along," Aunt Millie groused.

"Of course they will," Lacey chirped. Excitement welled up inside. She'd always had to endure lonely holiday meals with the cook at the academy. This would be her first time to have a true holiday feast. "And so will Stone Creedon and Chaps Smythe. They sit and play dominoes and checkers with Swede and Ebenezer Wilson every day. I can't abide the thought that they'd feel left out."

"Child, you're talking yourself into a heap of work." Aunt Millie shook her head. "With my arm like it is, I'm barely helping out as is. You try cooking a whole fancy feast, and—"

"We'll all pitch in," Jeff said.

Flashing him a grateful smile, Lacey said, "So it's settled."

❧

Jeff whistled under his breath. "Wow."

Lacey beamed. "Isn't this fun?"

"You outdid yourself." He stared at the dining room. She'd pushed two tables together to form a big square. A snowy tablecloth covered it, and she'd folded napkins on the plates to form fancy fan-shaped designs. Apples, nuts, and ribbons cascaded out of a pair of cornucopias as a centerpiece.

"I'll have to ask you to light the candles just before we begin. I can't reach them."

"Sure." He'd come over early to help out—or as Millie put it, "rein her in." Lacey got some crazy notion that this was supposed to be a seven-course meal. For the past week, he and Millie kept cutting down Lacey's grand plan and nixed over half of the menu items.

It started when Lacey asked his preference between oyster bisque and some other fishy-sounding soup. "To be honest, I've got my mouth set for turkey."

"Naturally, we'll have turkey. I'm talking about the soup course, though."

Millie had chimed in. "Why waste time making that? They won't care. Give the men what they want."

"Very well." Lacey sighed, then brightened. "Then let's discuss appetizers. I was thinking how lovely it would be to have an assortment of—"

"Turkey, child. The men want turkey."

"And stuffing," Jeff had tacked on. "I couldn't care less about a bunch of little morsels. I'm saving all my room for the good stuff."

Good stuff. He hadn't known just what that meant to Lacey, but now he was finding out. "Did you sleep at all last night?"

"A little." She bustled toward the kitchen and over to the stove, where she lifted the lid on a pot and gave the contents a quick stir. "Aunt Millie, if you'd put the baskets of rolls on the table, I'd appreciate it. Jeff, would you please move this pot of potatoes onto the table so I can use the burner for something else?"

Hefting the pot, he asked, "Want me to drain the water?"

"Not just yet. It'll keep them hot until I mash them." She set a coffeepot on to percolate, then opened the oven. The nearly overpowering aroma of turkey burst into the room, but Lacey reached beside the huge pan and pulled out another dish. She opened the lid, drizzled butter atop yams, and sprinkled brown sugar over it all.

Jeff's stomach rumbled. "I'm not going to be able to wait another half hour to eat."

"Yes, you will." She waggled her spoon at him. "I have this all scheduled, and no one is going to destroy my plan."

"Oh, give the man a cookie," Millie laughed as she came back in.

"It'll spoil his appetite."

"I'm not a child."

Lacey paused and looked up at him. Her lips parted, then closed. Though she'd already been rosy from the heat of the stove, her color heightened. "No one could mistake you for a child. Forgive me."

"It'll cost you a cookie." He winked. "You can buy me off cheaply."

"Spoken like a true friend," Millie said as she pulled butter from the icebox.

"Friends and family—that's what today's all about." Tears sheened Lacey's eyes, turning them into glistening pools of gold. "Being thankful to the Lord with those we love."

A knock sounded at the door. She smoothed her skirts and went to answer it. Millie watched her go, then murmured, "I didn't figure it out till last night. Did you know that gal hasn't had a family Thanksgiving since her mama passed on? She was only six. Ever since then, she's been stuck at that snooty school. It's why she's so dead set to make today perfect."

"Then let's make her dreams come true."

⁂

The turkey skidded off the platter and onto the table. Ebenezer Wilson growled, stabbed the bird with the carving fork and knife, and wrestled it back onto the platter, then proceeded to hack the beautiful golden brown bird into unidentifiable chunks.

"You made succotash!" Jeff shot Lacey a huge smile as he lifted the lid off the dish. "My favorite!"

"I'm glad." Well, at least that went well.

"What's this in the dressing?" Stone Creedon stabbed at something with his fork.

"Oysters," Lacey said as a sinking feeling swamped her. Didn't Texans use oysters in their stuffing?

"I say!" Chaps Smythe reached over, speared the oyster straight off Stone's plate, and gulped it down. "Excellent! I haven't had oyster stuffing in years." He then proved his liking for the dish by scooping almost a third of the bowl onto his plate.

Rafe kept trying to coax Peony to have a little taste of each item as the dishes were passed around the table. Lacey secretly thought it a marvel her friend wasn't abjectly ill just from the sight of her husband's heaping plate with gravy dripping off the edge. Lacey tried to distract herself by helping serve Aunt Millie.

Finally, everything had been around the table, and Lacey relaxed. She promised herself she was going to enjoy today. Picking up her knife and fork, she managed a smile. Everything wasn't exactly picture-perfect, but everyone seemed content.

Bang, bang, bang.

Chapter 8

Lacey jumped at the sound, turned, and tamped down a groan. Ticks McGee and Jay Harris both peered through the window.

"I'll take care of this." Jeff rose and headed toward the door. He opened it and said in a firm tone, "The diner's closed today."

"It can't be," Jay Harris said.

"Oh, I smell turkey." Ticks sounded somewhere between heaven and torture.

Memories of lonely holiday meals washed over Lacey. She rushed over to the door as tears filled her eyes. "Please join us. I should have thought to invite you. I'm so sorry."

"You don't have to do this," Jeff said in a low tone. His

large body still blocked the door.

Lacey looked up at him. "I want to. Everyone deserves to belong and be wanted."

"Okay." He brushed her tears away. "You men wipe your feet."

Rafe came over. "And go wash off that bay rum, McGee. My wife can't take it."

Hours later, everyone wandered off. Lacey was up to her elbows in water, and Jeff dried the dishes. "We ran out of stuffing," she said.

"So what?" Aunt Millie awkwardly poured the last bit of cranberry jelly from a bowl into a Ball-Mason jar. "If you wanna squawk, then talk about what Eb did to the bird."

"No harm done," Jeff said blandly. "It still tasted great."

"I should have made another pie."

"There was plenty until we got company," Aunt Millie said in a wry tone.

Heavy-hearted, Lacey nodded. "I should have planned better. I should have invited them and made more." She glanced at Jeff. "I'm sorry you didn't get any pie."

"I had my dessert before supper—remember the cookies?"

"You're a gallant man, Jeffrey Wilson."

His big hands stopped drying a platter. Eyes steady as could be, he studied her and said, "You're every inch a fine lady, Lacey Mather—but more than that, you're a good woman. This Thanksgiving was unforgettable."

"Thank you. I've never received a sweeter compliment. I wanted to do something special so we could all look back fondly. Years from now, I know I'll always treasure this day that I spent with you."

"There can be more of them, you know." He reached over and brushed a bubble from her sleeve.

Her hands sank to the bottom of the sink, and her heart went right along with them. "No. I'll go back to Boston soon." Forcing a smile, she tacked on, "Where I'll even have a white Christmas."

❧

"Stubborn woman." Jeff brought the hammer down again to punctuate his opinion. What was wrong with Lacey? Couldn't she see her life was here in Cut Corners?

"We came to talk sense into you," Uncle Eb said from beyond the rail.

Jeff glowered at him and the other three meddling men. "What now?"

"You can't let Lacey Mather go back East," Chaps declared. "It's simply unacceptable."

"You're thinking with your belly," Jeff said. It irritated him that these men only cared about Lacey because she could cook. Didn't they see past that? Couldn't they understand that she deserved to be loved and have a family surrounding her?

"Plenty of young bucks around Cut Corners. Every last one of 'em thinks she's a fine catch," Stone Creedon said.

"Better make a quick move," Swede advised.

"I think we've said enough," Uncle Eb declared. He nudged Chaps. "Let's get back to the game. I'm going to whup you like a rented mule."

"Pride goeth before destruction, and an haughty spirit before a fall." Chaps inspected him for a moment through his monocle—an action intended to lend impact to his words. The old ranger then straightened his shoulders and marched out with the others close on his tail.

Uncle Eb stuck his head back into the smithy. "Son, don't let pride keep you from love. She might well be a great cook, but the truth is, since she's come, you're a different man. Puts me of a mind on how I was once I met my wife. When God gives you that blessing, you have to accept it."

After he left, Jeff shoved the iron back into the fire. *Lord, I feel like that bar—You're going to have to heat me, bend me, and hammer me into the man Lacey needs. You're going to have to bend her spirit, too, because she's so dead set on taking a different path.*

❧

Dear Mrs. Delphine,

I deeply regret to inform you that my great-aunt's health is still unstable. Her physician recommends that I remain with her until the New Year. Please forgive me for any inconveniences my absence causes you and the plans you've made for the holiday season.

Sincerely,
Lacey Marie Mather

Ticks read the telegraph and cleared his throat. "I'd be honored to have you sit with me for the Christmas Day service."

"Your offer is most kind, Mr. McGee, but I don't believe that would be wise." Lacey tried to speak gently. He was a nice man—but not the one for her. "When a reply comes, please give it to my aunt. I'll be out running errands."

"Sewing with Peony again?"

Lacey gasped. How did he know where she went and what she did? The very notion that he kept track of her made chills run down her spine. "Good day, Mr. McGee." She set payment for the telegram on the counter and left with what Madame termed "purposeful decorum."

Bless her, Peony had offered to have them sew back in

Aunt Millie's parlor. After the fiery debacle the last time, Lacey knew nothing but relief that her friend understood the necessity of keeping close watch over the situation. Lacey stepped foot into Peony's place and asked, "What shall I carry?"

"Rafe already took it over. He refuses to let me lift a thing." She cast a look across the street. "Lionel Sager hired me to make a dress for Vivian for Christmas. Just wait until you see—it's a blue, button-down wool."

"What a wonderful surprise! I can't keep anything from Aunt Millie. She's more curious than any cat, so you know what I did?"

"No, what?"

"I sent away to Boston for Christmas gifts!"

"How clever of you!" They stepped out onto the boardwalk.

"She's a clever gal, all right," Swede declared as he hunkered over the checkerboard. "I'm thinking I ought to challenge her to a game."

Stone snorted. "You just want someone new to beat."

Peony dipped her head and kissed Ebenezer Wilson on his weathered cheek. "I'm going to Millie's to sew, Father. If anyone comes to the shop, you can tell them where I am."

"Okay, darlin'." The old man smiled at his daughter-in-law, then patted her hand. "Don't work too hard."

"I won't let her." Lacey held Peony's arm and led her down the boardwalk. The genuine affection between Peony and Eb never failed to touch her deeply. She couldn't recall a single time when her own father had given her the merest scrap of attention. "The Lord has blessed you so much," she said to her friend.

"Hasn't He?" Peony beamed. She glanced around and lowered her voice. "I confess to being selfish, though. I've been praying, Lacey. I've asked God to keep you here so I'll have a friend when my time comes."

Lacey's step faltered. "Now, Peony—"

"I put it in God's hands. Neither of us is going to snatch it back." She continued to sashay along the gritty boardwalk. "I do declare, I believe that you, Vivian, and I are the only ones who sweep in front of our establishments."

"You're trying to change the subject."

"And you'll humor me because you're such a dear." Peony's laughter tinkled on the crisp air.

"Ladies!" Ticks McGee looked like a crane as he lifted his knees high to pick his way across the rutted road. He waved a piece of paper. "Telegram!" Face flushed, he stood before them and straightened his shoulders. "Dear Miss Mather—"

"I'm able to read the telegram, Mr. McGee."

Ticks ignored Lacey and read, " 'I shall hold your aunt in my prayers. Please extend my wishes for complete recovery. Your loving care surely blesses her. I've arranged for someone to stay with those who are unable to go home for Christmas. Looking forward to seeing you in January. Sincerely, Amanda Delphine.' Isn't that the finest news? You'll be staying here in Cut Corners!"

"Only through Christmas, Mr. McGee." Lacey held out her hand.

Instead of giving her the telegram, he shook her hand!

Thunderstruck by his forward behavior, Lacey stood frozen to the planks beneath her feet.

"Miss Mather isn't a water pump, Ticks." Jeff sauntered over and slapped Ticks on the back in a friendly way.

"She's staying through Christmas!"

Jeff looked straight into Lacey's eyes. "That," he rumbled in a thrillingly deep tone, "is the best news of the year."

⟡

"What is that racket?" Jeff rolled out of bed and yanked on his jeans. Shrugging into his shirt, he headed toward the door. The instant he realized what and where the commotion came from, he jogged toward Millie's.

"Shoo fly, don't bother me," one of the cowhands from

the Gustavson spread sang.

"Stop that caterwauling," Jeff snapped.

"Shoo fly, don't bother me." The cowboy took his hat from where he'd been holding it so earnestly over his heart and flapped it toward Jeff.

"Leave the man alone. He's shher–en–ading hishh lady love," one of the other cowboys slurred drunkenly.

Lacey Mather deserved far better than a penniless saddle tramp and his sotted sidekicks. Irritated, Jeff barked, "Hush. It's the middle of the night!"

"It's called a moonlight ser–a–nade. It's romantic." The cowboy glowered at him.

"That shhong didn't work. Try a differ'n one," one of his pals urged. "What 'bout 'The Bear Went Over the Mountain'?"

"I'm partial to 'Turkey in the Schtraw,'" another hiccupped.

"'Old Dan Tucker' or 'Little Brown Jug,'" a third suggested.

"Those ain't romantic," the suitor snapped.

"And 'Shoo Fly' was?" Jeff couldn't believe this ridiculous scene. "It's the middle of the night. Leave the poor girl alone."

"You just want the girl for yourself."

The accusation hung in the crisp air. Jeff widened his stance, stared at the men, and asked in a very still tone, "What if I do?"

Chapter 9

W hat if I do?" Jeff's words seeped into the room, and Lacey muffled her gasp. Awakening to the so-called serenade had been surprise enough for the night. An embarrassing surprise. Lacey hadn't opened the curtains or the door because she didn't want to encourage such nonsense. Aunt Millie slept through the whole thing, but Lacey didn't delude herself into believing that meant the rest of Cut Corners would do likewise. By tomorrow, she'd have to face all of the diners' smirks and teasing comments.

But now, Jeff put himself on the line. Of all the bachelors in this crazy town, only he hadn't pestered her. Oh, he'd definitely had his share of observations regarding her would-be suitors. Never once did he stoop to being cruel or unkind about those men, and he made it clear he found her worthy of such attention, however bumbling it might be. But he respected her ambition to go back to Boston and become a teacher. He alone hadn't asked her to change to suit his pleasure.

Such chivalry, she thought. *He's putting himself between those men and me. And honorable! He didn't tell a lie. They asked him, but he only responded back with a hypothetical question.*

Lacey leaned against the wall and drew her robe about herself more tightly. *It's all so confusing. I don't understand these men. I ought to be happy to go back to Boston, back to the company of genteel women whom I understand and young girls in need of guidance.*

I ought to, but I'm not sure I am.

❧

"Come back in half an hour." Millie slammed the door in Jeff's face.

He stood out in the rain with a huge scuttle of coal. The last thing he wanted to do was traipse across the street again, then interrupt his morning's work to redeliver this fuel. Irritated, he booted the door open and groused, "I'm a busy man."

Feminine chatter suddenly stilled, save one high-pitched squeal.

Jeff stopped dead in his tracks.

Peony stood on crate, and Lacey knelt on the floor, pinning the hem of her dress. They'd stuffed a pillow or something under the skirt to allow for Peony's increasing size due to her delicate condition.

Peony let out a choked sob.

Lacey jumped to her feet and stood at an angle to block Jeff's view. "Why, Jeff. Yes, you are a busy man. No use in holding you back." Her voice stayed quite calm. All of those years of training served her well. "If you'll please fill the stove, I'd appreciate it. Oh, and I've been making gingerbread. It's not iced yet, but you're welcome to cut yourself a piece."

"Don't mind if I do." Given that reprieve, he hotfooted it into the kitchen. It always struck him as silly for everyone to pretend to ignore the fact that the Lord was blessing a woman with a child. Nonetheless, Peony tried so hard to observe every societal dictate. Given her background, Jeff understood why it was so important to her. Lacey—well, she'd salvaged a bad situation with her smooth thinking.

Making it a point to be noisy so they'd be able to track his whereabouts, Jeff dumped the coal, clattered around to cut a huge chunk of the gingerbread, and shouted, "Thanks, Lacey." He strode through the diner and half slammed the door to reassure them he wasn't about to scandalize them with his presence again.

"What you got there?" Stone Creedon squinted at him.

"Gingerbread."

The old ranger spraddled closer and tore off a huge portion of the fragrant treat. "Guess it'll have to do. I was hopin' you'd bring out cookies."

"You know how Lacey is about those."

"She does?"

Jeff gave Stone a quizzical look. Given an opportunity, the old guy usually talked enough to explain his odd mishearings. Confronting him with them or asking him to use his ear horn only got him riled.

"Mayhap she oughtta git her some new shoes then. Or socks. Good cotton ones—not them silk kind."

"Jeff." Rafe sauntered up. He cocked his brow and grabbed for what little gingerbread remained. "We need to talk."

"Sure do. Jeff, tell Rafe all about it. He can talk sense into Peony, and then she can make Lacey see reason."

"What's happening with Lacey?"

Stone brushed crumbs from his droopy mustache. "She's got bad toes." He perked up. "Tell you what. Me and the others, we'll come serve lunch and supper today. Thataway, Lacey can soak her feet."

"Great idea," Rafe said. He and Jeff watched as Stone headed toward his cronies. "Are you going to fetch Doc Winston?"

"I don't think there's any need. Stone just jumbled up what I said. So what do we need to talk about?"

"Word around town is you have Gustavson's cowboys sore at you. I saw the tail end of what happened last night, and I know you too well. If you were just trying to get rid of them, they'll be back and pester her half to death. If you're serious, then you need to make it clear to everyone that the little lady is yours."

Jeff leaned against the diner's wall. "Rafe, convincing them isn't going to be the hard part."

❦

"Have you seen the sign-up list for the bachelors' dinner?" Peony asked Vivian as they decorated the church.

"No. Why?"

"Because I didn't know there were that many bachelors in Cut Corners. Gordon Brooks even signed up, so the Tankard will be closed!" Lacey tacked up a swag of pine. "I'll need to order more beef."

"Just tell me how much," Vivian murmured as she shoved her slipping spectacles higher on her nose. "I'll make sure we have it in the mercantile for you."

"That's not what I was talking about." Peony let out an exasperated sound. "Millie put out the list, and the page was almost full before lunch ended. Jeff wasn't at lunch, so when he caught wind of that list, he went and put his name at the very top in huge, bold letters."

Vivian clasped her hands over her heart. "Lacey, I'm sure the man has a tendresse for you."

If only he did. Lacey shook her head. "No, no. He's just being a very good friend. He's trying to shoo away all of those men so I don't have to deal with any more awkward proposals."

"I've never gotten a single proposal," Vivian said quietly as she lifted her hem and carefully got onto a stepladder.

"Neither had I until I came here," Lacey said crisply. "And I wouldn't consider any of the offers I've received as being serious. Those men want a cook. If I ever marry, it'll be because the man loves me, not because he loves my suppers."

Erik Olson entered the sanctuary. "But your cookies— they could win any man's heart." His light blue eyes danced with a teasing light. "I will settle, though, to have you as my sister in Christ."

"That's sweet, Erik," Peony said. "What do you have?"

"I heard you ladies were decorating the church, so I made this. It's the Advent wreath. Vivian, you have the right colors of the candles at the store, ja?"

"I'm sure we do." Vivian scrambled down the stepladder and over to him. "Wouldn't that look positively splendid in front of the pulpit?"

Erik smiled and turned to Lacey. "I am supposed to ask you a question. The bachelors' dinner—Ebenezer wishes to know if widowers are also invited."

"He never went before," Vivian said.

"Lacey was not doing the cooking then." Erik chuckled. "Please do not take this wrong, but Millie's cooking—it is bad. We all love her, so we took turns eating at the diner to make her feel good."

"She is lovable, isn't she?" Lacey looked at all of them. "So are you. What you all have here in Cut Corners is so special—you all care for one another."

"You could stay, you know," Peony said.

"Ja, you should stay." Erik nodded.

"Maybe she wants more adventure in her life," Vivian said. "Ticks told me a woman is a telephone operator in Boston now."

"Boston is altogether different from Cut Corners." Lacey dipped her head and pretended to concentrate on binding the pine boughs to form the next swag. The school in Boston had her pledge, but Cut Corners had her heart. *Lord Jesus, what am I to do? Please show me Your will.*

Jeff couldn't stand it anymore. He'd barely endured the bachelors' pot roast luncheon. Lacey turned the whole thing into a veritable feast. Oh, she'd gone way overboard—and though she'd had Mary Jo Heath, Vivian Sager, and even the young Widow Phelps there to help her serve, the men barely spared those single women a glance.

Every last one of those men fancied himself in love with Lacey. Jeff knew better. He alone suffered that particular malady. Lacey and the girls were picking up the dessert plates, but none of the men took the hint to leave.

Jeff wasn't about to depart until every last man had vacated the premises.

Lacey finally halted at the door to the kitchen and clasped her hands just below her bosom. The pose came naturally—it wasn't meant to be coy, but it drove Jeff daft. When she stood like that, it called his attention to her tiny waist.

"Gentlemen, you're all invited to return this evening at seven. The whole community is welcome for a Christmas dessert reception."

The men all rumbled their delight.

Jeff stood up. "The lady's being polite, men. Now scat so she can get things ready." The guests trundled out, but Jeff's hackles rose when he spied Harold Myers slipping Lacey a note. Then and there, Jeff knew what he had to do.

Chapter 10

Place looks awful fancy." Aunt Millie's grousing tone didn't sting one bit because of the wide smile she wore.

"So do we," Lacey said. "Your new dress is marvelous!"

Aunt Millie ran her left hand down the skirts of the blue delft print. "Never had someone give me a store-bought dress. It's like putting a wreath of flowers on a mule."

"Nonsense!" Lacey pulled her Sunday-best apron over her new Christmas gown. For tonight, she'd attached a collar with little green sprigs embroidered along the edge and added a wide green sash. The festive look matched her mood. "I hope we have enough food."

"As much as the men ate today at lunch, they shouldn't be able to wedge another bite in sideways for three days,"

Aunt Millie said. She sighed. "I may as well confess, I don't blame 'em. I guess we've all grown accustomed to your eastern recipes. My pot roast never tasted like that."

"Her recipes aren't all she brought with her from Boston," Jeff said as he let himself in. He held the door wide open. "Take a look."

Lacey tilted her head to look around him. "Snow!"

"Yup." He grinned. "Merry Christmas."

"Oh, snow!" She dashed past him and out into the gently falling flakes and turned her face upward. "Thank You, Jesus! Now it really feels like Christmas!"

"Here." Jeff wrapped something around her.

Lacey glanced down at the soft white merino wool shawl and gasped. "This is beautiful, Jeff."

"Merry Christmas. I figured if we didn't get snow, you'd still have something white falling onto your hair and shoulders."

"That's the most thoughtful thing anyone has ever done for me."

"Lacey. . ." Jeff turned her toward himself.

"Hoo—oo—ey! It's snowing!" Stone Creedon shouted as he and the other old rangers ambled up. "Hope you got lotsa hot coffee on the stove, missy."

"I do. Please, come in." Lacey wished Jeff hadn't been interrupted. He'd looked very intent. Then, too, she'd wanted to tell him her news. Would it make him half as happy as it made her?

"I'm gonna drink a pot all of my own," Stone continued to ramble.

Lacey cast Jeff an apologetic look. She needed to assume her duties as a hostess.

He heaved a sigh. "Go on."

All of Cut Corners turned out for the Christmas Eve dessert reception. Lacey wove in and out of the crowd, chatting with her friends and neighbors while setting out more pies, tarts, cakes, and cookies.

Happiness bubbled in her like the coffee perking on the stove. She'd asked God for direction, and He'd been faithful. The letter from Amanda Delphine today released her from her commitment to the Ladies Academie. From now on, she'd have a home—here, with Aunt Millie.

Jeff followed her into the kitchen. "Want me to take that cake there on into the other room?"

"Oh no." She smiled. "Tomorrow is Rafe's birthday. I made that cake so we could celebrate."

"Come here." Jeff dragged her from the kitchen to the parlor.

"But everyone—"

"Everyone can wait." He cupped her face in his rough

hands. "Lacey, I've tried my best to respect your wishes. I know you want to go back to that fancy school, but I can't let you go. I want you to stay here. With me. Lacey, I'm not good with words. What I'm trying to say is, I love you. I want you to marry me."

"This is all so sudden." Madame drilled all of her young ladies to stall for a moment with that phrase so they could gather their thoughts. Lacey laughed. She didn't want to pause. "Oh, Jeffrey. How can you say you're not good with words? Those are the best words I've ever heard. Nothing would make me happier than to stay in Cut Corners and be your wife."

His eyes lit with joy.

"I received a letter from Mrs. Delphine today. She said the other woman is working out well, and if I didn't mind, she'd like to allow her to keep the position. I'm free to stay here, with you."

"And I'm not going to let you go." He pressed a swift kiss on her cheek, then grabbed her wrist and dragged her back into the diner. "I have an announcement! Lacey's going to marry me!"

Everyone cheered.

Old Ebenezer Wilson slapped him on the back. "No time like the present. What do you say, Parson Clune?"

"It's a fine time to be married."

Everyone hastened across to the church. Peony quickly untied Lacey's apron and removed the green-trimmed collar. Vivian pulled a length of elegant white lace from her pocket. "Here. And I have a bouquet, too."

"You do?" Lacey stared at her in amazement.

"Of course I do. Jeff came to the mercantile today to buy your ring. I thought you'd probably get married after church tomorrow, but I brought everything over to the sanctuary tonight before your party."

The sanctuary was nearly freezing, but the crispness in the air made the pine boughs more fragrant. "It's too cold to sit in the pews," Parson Clune decided. "Everyone stand around the edges in a big circle."

In a matter of minutes, everyone held a bayberry candle. By that glow, Uncle Eb escorted Lacey to the altar.

Solemn vows, a kiss, and then Jeff swept Lacey into his arms. "This is the merriest Christmas since Christ came!"

"And there's a wedding cake back at the diner," Aunt Millie declared. "It's Rafe's gift to the bride and groom."

Jeff carried Lacey outside and halted as snowflakes danced about them. She snuggled close. "I love you."

"Now that's an even bigger miracle than snow for Christmas."

"Hundreds of years ago, God touched our souls with the gift of His Son. Tonight He touched our hearts again with His gift of love for one another. I'm in your arms, Jeffrey. I'm home."

"Welcome home." He dipped his head and sealed his greeting with a kiss.

BROWN SUGAR COOKIES

2 cups light brown sugar
1 cup melted butter
3 eggs
¼ cup milk
1 tbsp. vanilla
1 tsp. baking soda
5–5½ cups flour

Mix ingredients in order given. Add just enough flour to make dough firm enough to roll. Cut into shapes as desired. Decorate with raisins or brown sugar, bake at 350 degrees for 8–10 minutes or until edges are lightly browned.

CATHY MARIE HAKE

Cathy Marie Hake is a Southern California native who loves her work as a nurse and Lamaze teacher. She and her husband have a daughter, a son, and two dogs, so life is never dull or quiet. Cathy Marie considers herself a sentimental packrat, collecting antiques and Hummel figurines. She otherwise keeps busy with reading, writing, and bargain hunting. Cathy Marie's first book was published by Heartsong Presents in 2000 and earned her a spot as one of the readers' favorite new authors. Since then, she's written several other novels, novellas, and gift books. You can visit her online at www.CathyMarieHake.com.

A Letter to Our Readers

Dear Readers:

In order that we might better contribute to your reading enjoyment, we would appreciate your taking a few minutes to respond to the following questions. When completed, please return to the following: Fiction Editor, Barbour Publishing, Inc., P.O. Box 719, Uhrichsville, OII 44683.

1. Did you enjoy reading *Texas Christmas Brides*?
   ❑ Very much—I would like to see more books like this.
   ❑ Moderately—I would have enjoyed it more if _____
   _____

   _____

2. What influenced your decision to purchase this book?
   (Check those that apply.)
   ❑ Cover   ❑ Back cover copy   ❑ Title   ❑ Price
   ❑ Friends   ❑ Publicity   ❑ Other

3. Which story was your favorite?
   ❑ *The Marrying Kind*   ❑ *Here Cooks the Bride*

4. Please check your age range:
   ❑ Under 18   ❑ 18–24   ❑ 25–34
   ❑ 35–45   ❑ 46–55   ❑ Over 55

5. How many hours per week do you read? _____

Name _____

Occupation _____

Address _____

City_____ State_____ Zip_____

E-mail_____